Shatterpoint:

An Amari Kato Novella

By B.R. Michaels

Once Upon A Queer Publishing LLC

Published by Once Upon A Queer Publishing LLC
ISBN: 9798992598476 (paperback)
Printed in the United States of America

Cover design by Once Upon A Queer Publishing LLC

SHATTERPOINT
An Amari Kato Novella

Amari Kato turns a corner at breakneck speed and nearly runs straight into a pole before slipping around it. She weaves through pedestrians and jumps over or slides below any obstacles in her way. Her small size helps her in this instance, letting the thirteen-year-old escape her pursuers more quickly than she would otherwise. Her ram horns scrape the underside of a table as she drops down and past it.

The backpack, tightly strapped on, weighs heavily on her in more ways than one, especially as she notices the heads of people she passes turning in her direction. Are the guards still chasing her? How close?

She's been deaf for years now, and it still makes Amari's heart race in moments like this.

Thankfully, she has more than the standard five senses to rely on.

An instinctive warning is all she gets before she has to duck a flying net. It hits the wall where she had just been, and she feels the cement reverberating with the impact. She picks up the muffled noise of screams as alarmed bystanders flee.

The danger is mounting, and Amari keeps running through the streets of Castor's Merchant District as she follows the whims of her instincts. They've kept her out of the guard's claws so far. She has to slide beneath a cart as someone lunges from an alleyway.

How long can Amari keep this up? Relying so heavily on magic only works for so long before there's a steep price to pay. The girl already feels pain sprouting in her mind, a full-blown migraine all but imminent.

An urge to move in a specific direction comes over her so strongly that it nearly throws Amari off her feet. Instead of questioning the magically spurred idea, she ducks into the alleyway it leads her down.

Only to see a brick wall a dozen meters down. Too high for her to climb with the time she has, and she would have stopped running if her feet weren't practically being moved on their own. She closes her eyes as she approaches the wall at full speed—

—and then trips over a tree root, falling onto her face into a soft grass field.

She simply lies there for a moment, the juxtaposition of everything stalling her thoughts. Then Amari sits up urgently, looking at her new surroundings.

... It's decidedly not the Merchant District of Castor.

Directly ahead, a field stretches on for meters until it hits a line of shrubbery set against an iron-wrought fence. Looking around, it quickly becomes apparent that Amari is in some park. Hopefully not a private one, she thinks as she hurriedly stands up and dusts off her dark clothing.

The alleyway her magic powers led her to must have contained a naturally occurring portal of some kind to send her here. She's had brushes with them in the past before, but they're still considered rare events in the world. However, the city of Castor has more reported instances of phenomena like this than most places...

It has something to do with the wild ambient magic of the

city, which is one of the things that drew Amari to it. She stayed because finding places to sleep at night in Castor's Lower District was pretty simple. As long as you don't mind the city's strangeness.

Eyeing the empty park around her, Amari slinks out of the open field and into the tree line. It's not a great cover, she admits to herself as she sizes up the fence. By following it around, the girl is hoping to find the exit. With luck, the gates are unlocked.

As she walks and keeps an eye out for any onlookers, Amari reaches a hand back to check her bag. The backpack is secure, and all contents are safely inside despite the rough treatment the chase put it through. A sigh of relief escapes her, and she focuses on fixing her braid so she has something to do with her hands. It takes a minute to untangle all stray hairs entirely from her horns, and her sharp black nails threaten to cut into her head a few times in her haste.

The tension doesn't truly start leaving her frame until she spots an open gate, and a slight skip in her step shows up as she exits the park. Outside, the streets of Castor greet her, yet they look different from what she's used to. It is much better-maintained than the place she lives in. This must be the Upper District. Amari has only ever seen it from across the river that bisects the city.

Castor is a place rife with wild ambient magic, but the wealthier sector manages to pull off the image of being orderly. The streets' cobblestones are immaculately kept, polished to a sheen that reflects the ambient glow of floating lanterns. Amari has to admit to herself that it's strange to see a whole street full of perfectly functioning lights. These lanterns, held aloft by softly humming enchantments, radiate a cool, silvery light that illuminates the roads without casting harsh shadows. Their flickering flames appear as though they're alive, whispering faintly in a language only the most educated Scribes of the district might understand. Amari picks up the whispers, which means they're being telepathically sent straight to her mind, and she hurries past.

Grand estates line the streets, each surrounded by high wrought-iron gates etched with wards to deter unwanted guests. The manors themselves are gothic masterpieces, with soaring arches, stained-glass windows that shimmer with shifting magical patterns, and doorways framed by intricate carvings of celestial beings or mythical beasts. It's so picturesque that Amari looks away in disgust. Some things look too perfect to be real.

All around, the air smells faintly of incense and ozone, making her nose wrinkle. It's a byproduct of the protective spells that shield this district from the chaos and grime of the less fortunate sectors. The magical infrastructure here is flawless—fountains bubble with crystal-clear water that sparkles unnaturally in the moonlight, and subtle glamors keep the temperature mild regardless of the season. Even the chimneys of the wealthier homes emit no smoke, as many of these mansions are powered by bound elementals or arcane cores.

The Upper District exudes a blend of security and danger that has Amari bristling. This part of the city has no Rooftop Kings or smaller gangs lurking around the corners—just guards and lords.

Reminded of the guards chasing her just minutes before, Amari hastens in what she thinks is the way to the river. As long as she can cross to her home sector and avoid the small island that is the Merchant District, she's in the clear. The guards rarely venture far into the less wealthy parts of Castor. Even the tourists who come for Castor's reputation as the most haunted city in Esma are wary of the Lower District.

Ducking into a side street, Amari keeps a wary eye out for anyone who might look at her too long. Her facial markings are easy to identify her by, and she hopes she did a decent job of going unseen until right at the end. She's certainly been outed as a Nightblood, but with luck, her unique markings weren't cataloged. Amari doesn't have the money to buy a mask or headscarf, and thievery is what got her into this situation.

Shadows stretch ahead of her, and she notes the first cracked moon peeking above the horizon. Night will fall soon, making her escape all the easier. It also eases the aching of her head, as sensitive to the light as her eyes are. Most Nightbloods are waking up now, so Amari is the weird one in this respect. She just has no patience for a proper sleep schedule when she could be getting things done *now*.

The scent of the ocean hits her nose, making her smile. It shouldn't be far.

Keeping to the shadows, Amari weaves through the crowds on their way home from work or the ones just starting. The sound of the docks—always in motion, busy with all the ships that stop at the coastal city—begins to reach even her, and the tops of sails poke out above the buildings.

Even in the clean streets of this district, Amari gets a face full of the scent of fish and salt, making her heightened nose twitch. Finally coming into full view, the docks sprawl across the riverbank on both sides. Watching over the parked boats and managing the new arrivals is a full-time job. Patrols of guards walk by often, but they're also at their most distracted. Watching one kid isn't their priority when they have to be on the lookout for smugglers and their ilk.

Since darkness will fall soon, she figures that she'll find a hiding spot, wait a bit, and steal a rowboat to cross the river when no one's looking. Beats trying to cross one of the highly monitored and warded bridges. It's certainly easier to leave the Upper District than enter it, but she would still rather not try her luck again so soon.

Amari sneaks through the docks, making an effort not to rely too much on her magic after already using so much today.

The wooden planks of the piers are weathered but enchanted to resist decay, and they shimmer faintly with protective runes carved into their surfaces. Workers haul crates filled with magical goods—glowing crystals, enchanted herbs, and even caged elemental creatures that hiss or flicker within their confines. These crates are stacked beside more mundane cargo: barrels of spices, bolts of fine silk, and crates of exotic fruits.

Some other children come by the docks just to get a peek at what's being brought in, and Amari pretends to be one of them as she passes by. To be fair, many of the goods are interesting, even if she doesn't want to call attention to herself by showing *too* much interest.

Docked along the piers are an array of ships. Some have sails made of enchanted silk that ripple with colors even when there's no wind, while others are powered by glowing crystal cores embedded in their hulls, pulsing faintly like heartbeats. A few are living vessels—wooden ships grown from magical trees, their masts branching like real trunks and their hulls creaking as if breathing. Sailors flit around, carrying out various acts of maintenance.

The river runs beneath her feet and stretches a kilometer out to the other bank, its waters glowing faintly with bioluminescent plankton enchanted to illuminate the depths. Strange fish with translucent fins dart beneath the surface, leaving trails of shimmering light. The water is calm, protected by a series of ancient magical wards etched into towering stone breakwaters that curve protectively around the docks. These wards hum faintly with power even from a distance, reverberating through Amari's body. They cast a soft golden shimmer across the waves, keeping dangerous sea creatures at bay.

She finds a pile of empty crates to bunker down between, prepared to move if necessary. Hopefully, this will be a good place to hide for the next hour or two as night falls.

Bored within moments, Amari pulls her backpack off and discreetly opens it to get a peek at the contents. The package seems like such a glaringly suspicious thing inside. Just knowing what it contains without looking makes her clutch the bag tightly to her chest. Depending on what she does next, Amari could finally live comfortably for the first time in years, or...

Or achieve something more important.

What does she value more, her survival or her revenge?

The conflicting desires war inside her, letting time slip by like sand from her fingers as the second moon rises. Lights brighten as the darkness grows, and the bustle of the docks takes a shadier turn with it.

Amari hardly pays attention to the world around her until someone leans against a crate she's hiding behind. The feeling of the wood straining under the new weight signals to her that they're there before she even tries to peek. At her low vantage point, she can see two Sky Lords—easily identified by their wings—standing around outside her spot. It feels like a hand is squeezing her throat. What does she do? They're mouths are moving, but whatever they're saying is far too low for her to parse, and they seem armed from the look of them.

Not that someone needs to be visibly armed to be dangerous. It's just that the people who can blast walls of fire or uproot trees aren't usually skulking on random docks at night.

After a minute, a new person joins them, but she can instantly tell something is wrong. The third is a man wearing a suit that's too nice to be associated with the other two ruffian types, and his purple eyes dart around nervously.

Amari can see a lot from their body language alone. The two Sky Lords are clearly the ones with power in this dynamic, posturing obviously in a way that highlights their weapons, while the third subtly leans away. They're all but crowding the third man like they're demanding his wallet. He's likely being threatened into something. Maybe the winged men are smugglers?

Except that smugglers are relatively established in coastal cities in this country, and this seems rather... Not amateur. Amari has just seen smugglers with much more refined practices. They often have legitimate businesses to cover the illicit. This is more like something to happen in a Lower District back alley than for the docks on this side of the river. Most criminals here wear suits.

She understands when one of the Sky Lords turns more toward her. Amari has to stop herself from ducking away in case he turns around and catches a glimpse of a tattoo that peeks out of the man's sleeve. For someone from the Lower District, it's a very distinct tattoo. One she often sees painted on the sides of buildings.

A pair of wings wrapped around a cannon. It's meant as a mockery of the sigils official lords put on banners and rings.

It represents the Rooftop King and his gang, who have overrun her sector. The man, who is shrouded in rumors that Amari puts little faith in, is a violent gang leader known for his unique brand of cruelty. Like these men, he's a Sky Lord, and the king specializes in mental magics, such as mind control, reading, and the like.

She's learned all sorts of tales about what he can do. Amari is disinclined to believe most of them—controlling the whole district would take more power than any mortal human can hold—but even the weakest mentalist can cause irreversible damage. It doesn't even matter if they know what they're doing.

Amari herself has an aptitude for telepathy and potential for mind control, but most of the ways it's used leave a bitter taste in her mouth. Mostly, she bolsters her mental shields and minds her business.

More importantly, these two Sky Lords here mean the Rooftop King is expanding his reach. Rather boldly. The only conclusion Amari can come to about this development is that it will negatively impact the Lower District, regardless of the man's success. If he fails, he'll take it out on them, or there will be a violent power vacuum. If he succeeds in any way, the Upper District will panic and bring the hammer of 'justice' down on them. Lose-lose situation.

Amari carefully shuffles back out of sight, going over plans on how to prepare for whatever upcoming conflict will unfold. There are some people she knows who she can warn... Maybe she could sell the information to someone.

No, that would draw too much attention. Better to only share this with individuals she knows.

The illicit meeting is wrapped quickly; whatever the three are discussing—likely the Rooftop King threatening a merchant into compliance—is done and over with as the third broken moon rises above the horizon.

Amari waits for them all to leave, counts to a hundred, and then back down to zero before exiting her hiding spot. Despite being awake for twelve hours already, a small part of her feels better now than in the daylight. Unfortunately, it's drowned out by the tiredness that comes from using a lot of her power in a short time.

Because Amari is walking the line of magical exhaustion already, the sharp warning that strikes her like a lightning bolt comes too late for her to react.

The girl is scrambling back to her hiding spot when sharp pain erupts in her right shoulder, wrenching a strangled shout from her. Instinctively, Amari drops to the ground with all her weight, like a puppet with its strings cut. It causes whatever has dug into her shoulder to be harshly ripped out as she ducks and rolls against the damp wooden piers. Ignoring the agony of a torn wound for a moment, Amari turns to look at what has attacked her.

She immediately registers it as some sort of animal before realizing her naivety. The thing that flies up and perches on the crates to loom above her is not a wild animal. It resembles a small, dragon-like creature, no larger than a hawk, with an elongated, serpentine body that allows it to move with eerie grace as it stalks closer from atop the crates. Its leathery wings are translucent, veined with faintly glowing lines of crimson and violet, reminiscent of blood vessels pulsing with magic. The wings are what give it away for Amari. She's read about how, when in flight, the glow dims, allowing the creature to meld seamlessly into the shadows.

A mage's familiar. *Specifically,* she thinks with a sinking stomach, *one of the Rooftop King's many creatures.*

Its scales are jet-black and shimmer faintly in low light, like oil on water, making it almost invisible in the darkness except to her sharp eyes. Still, it must have been impossible to see from her low hiding spot. And she had left its safety before the familiar ended its surveillance. Careless. Stupid.

Amari is struck more by the familiar's eyes, which are its most striking features: multifaceted like a fly's but glowing faintly with an eerie gold light. These eyes can see in complete darkness and track magical auras, allowing them to spy on both physical and magical dealings with equal efficiency. It always knew she was there, then.

If she survives this encounter, it'll go tattling to the Rooftop King immediately about the little eavesdropper. If she kills it —*somehow*—then its disappearance will create an investigation into what happened. She's pretty screwed no matter how this ends.

But first, Amari acknowledges as the familiar's haunches prepare to pounce much like a cat's, *I must survive.*

It leaps off its perch, diving, bombing her with talons, and maw gaping. She barely sidesteps the creature in time, feeling the brush of dark wings against her side. The movement brings a burst of pain from her shoulder, grounding her firmly in reality.

Amari leans into her power despite the approaching magical exhaustion as the familiar switches directions mid-air. Better to deal with the brutal migraine later than be dead now.

It charges straight at her again, twisting like a corkscrew as its speed increases. Time feels like it slows down as Amari frantically throws herself out of the way. She lands on her bad shoulder hard enough to rip a scream from her, and in the back of her mind, a timer is counting down.

The rough landing reminds her of the backpack strapped onto her, and the extra weight really isn't helping the agony of the wound.

... But it does give her an idea.

Before her thoughts can go further, Amari gets a thrill of alarm and rolls out of the way a split-second before the familiar brings its talon down on where her head just was. With a boldness she didn't know she had, the girl kicks out at the creature in this moment.

It does functionally nothing except to buy her time as the familiar is thrown off its balance. With those scales, even a spear would do little damage. However, Amari just needs *time.*

Forcing herself to her feet, she runs to the crates and pushes over a pile toward the familiar without hesitation at the loud noise it makes. As she thought, it only distracts the creature briefly from its prey. Amari uses that precious moment to open her backpack and rip through the packaging to grab a small tincture from the collection bundled together.

She pops the top and downs it before she can doubt herself, just as the familiar crashes through a crate with a furious yowl.

The effects are near instantaneous.

Water under the dock slows to an almost stop, the wind no longer ruffles her braid, and the familiar charging at her is moving at a snail's pace. All the while, Amari feels like her thoughts have sped up a mile a minute.

This is what happens when she drinks a magic amplifier? Amari had expected her instincts to heighten, not for time to *slow down* around her! And it is slowed down, she realizes with some distant amazement. The girl is not just sped up; she's actually affecting her environment.

She stands stunned for what might be a minute or could be all of a second before remembering she's in a life-or-death situation. The magic amplifier has a time limit, and once it fades, Amari is sure she'll be all but useless from exhaustion.

Already, she can feel a slow, creeping migraine. Not to mention the pain in her shoulder.

Solutions. Amari has no way to kill the familiar on hand. Its scales are too tough, and trying will waste the valuable time she has. Simply running away is an option, but a poor one. These things are made to track prey. So, she needs a place where she can wait it out or escape through. Another unstable portal hidden in an alleyway would be very helpful right now.

In the present, she skirts away from the creature moving in slow motion and scans the docks. Distantly, she thinks she sees a patrol of guards running this way, also slowed down.

"Great," Amari mutters. She glances away toward the ships resting in the water.

Wait. The water.

Crossing the river would make her a sitting target if her powers wear off before she reaches the other side, but the water itself...

Amari sighs heavily as she considers her next insane plan. With little precision, she takes off her jacket and wraps it tightly around her shoulder injury, wincing as she does. Then she jumps off the dock into the water. Interestingly, as soon as she touches the river, it starts losing the effects of her magic.

The river is a shock of coldness that she finds soothing against her aching head and burning shoulder. Amari basks in the relief for a moment before swimming under the docks, which leave her little room for air but conceal her well. She grimaces at the sight of what the underside of the wooden planks looks like. It's clear no one bothers to clean what they think no one will see.

Carefully, Amari turns her mental focus to her magic. With the amplifier, everything is so heightened that it's difficult to get a grasp of what she's doing exactly. It feels like she's taken hold of the very fabric of time itself. The thought sends a shiver down her spine that has nothing to do with the freezing water.

As best she can, she eases her grip on time. Letting it slip through her fingers like sand, feeling the wind pick up and the creature above her react to her sudden disappearance. Unsurprisingly, it quickly realizes she's under the docks, and it claws at the wooden planks in displeasure. Amari figures it must have some kind of heat vision and doesn't bother to suppress a mean smile.

The cold of a winter night in Castor would outright kill most humans. As a Nightblood, Amari finds it rather soothing, even if being underwater is not her preference. Better to leave that to the Sea Folk. She's lucky no one actually lives *in* Castor's river.

Above her head, she can see flecks of wood fall into the water as the dock shakes under the force of the familiar's fury. It desperately wants to dispatch the eavesdropper, yet knows getting into the water is practically a death sentence for the poor reptile. Amari is really feeling for it.

The docks start shaking with reverberations of many boots as the guard patrol arrives on the scene. Amari shrinks instinctively, hoping against hope that they blame the mess solely on the angry familiar. The shaking of the wood indicates *something* is going down. Logically, the guards are dealing with a hostile familiar and should be too busy to think of searching for anyone else.

Waiting is an exercise in agony, and she does it anyway. The shaking eventually stops. She waits for more and reaches into her magic to try to suss out any remaining threats nearby.

Amari only lets the relief wash over her when she confirms her powers sense nothing of note. Finally, *finally,* the girl pulls herself onto the docks and goes to steal a rowboat to cross the river. After the crazy night she's had, it's almost suspiciously easy as she uses the remaining amplifier's effects to navigate dangers and head home.

Reaching the Lower District elicits a strange cocktail of relief and wariness in Amari. This place is full of dangers, but they're ones she's familiar with. There's a strange comfort in that.

The streets of the less wealthy sector of Castor twist and sprawl like a living thing, drenched in a palpable sense of wildness and simmering magical instability. Here, magic is ever-present, but it is a far cry from the polished, controlled enchantments of the Upper District. Instead, it clings to the streets like an errant spark, unpredictable and often as dangerous as it is useful.

The narrow, uneven cobblestones are dimly illuminated by flickering street lamps, enchanted with weak, guttering flames of pale blue or sickly green. Many lamps have cracked or shattered, their magical cores leaking a faint, erratic glow that does more to deepen the shadows than dispel them.

Amari knows there's something haunted here. On some nights, she sees wraith-like wisps of residual magic drift aimlessly through the air, faintly shimmering as they coil like smoke around the legs of ignorant passersby before fading into the dark.

There's no such thing tonight, thankfully, and she traverses the district with hurried steps. The inevitable crash when the amplifier's effects wear off is an ever-present sword hanging over her head. She needs to be alone and safe—or as safe as one can be in this place—when that happens.

Amari avoids the working lights so she can stay in the darkness, and she stays clear of any evidence of people out after sunset. Most sensible residents have turned in by now, so she has no desire to meet who else is awake, even if it's likely to be another Nightblood who just woke up. Better safe than sorry and all that.

The tension in her frame doesn't leave even as she gets close to what has been her 'home' for some time now. Reaching the place is a trial in and of itself. She is in Castor's most run-down and abandoned sector, which is treacherous in more ways than one. The path to home begins with scaling the remains of a crumbled brick wall, then leaping across a series of dangerously unstable rooftops, each one missing tiles or entirely caved in. An old fire escape, its bolts rusted and groaning under the slightest weight, must be climbed to reach a narrow beam that extends across a yawning gap. The final approach requires shimmying along a ledge barely wider than a hand, with nothing but a three-story drop below.

What awaits her doesn't look worth the effort it took to reach it.

The shack is a crooked, lopsided structure of warped wood and peeling paint, its roof sagging under the weight of age and neglect. Jagged planks jut out at odd angles, forming a skeletal frame that seems barely capable of standing. Windows, long shattered, gape like hollow eyes, while the remnants of glass shards glimmer faintly in the moonlight. A rusted tin chimney pokes out at a strange tilt, and the door is a heavy metal contraption that Amari always has to push open with her whole body.

The shack seems to flicker faintly at the edges as though caught between dimensions. Sometimes, its silhouette appears sharp and solid; other times, it blurs, dissolving like smoke into the night. At rare moments, it disappears altogether, leaving only an eerie patch of empty air that feels wrong to look at, as if the space itself protests its absence.

Most people wouldn't dare to approach such a structurally and magically unstable building. However, for those daring— or desperate—enough to make the journey, the shack's perch offers a strange solace. Hidden among the city's ruins and seemingly forgotten by everyone else, it provides a shelter that no one else dares to claim, and its otherworldly nature means it often evades detection. Amari has been living in it for around two years. Its peculiarities barely phase her at this point.

She shoves the door open, steps through, and closes the thing by pushing a heavy wardrobe against it. Better than a lock someone can pick, she figures.

When she first arrived in the shack, the air was thick and still, heavy with the scent of damp wood and mildew. The floorboards creaked with every step, some so rotten that they sagged beneath even the lightest footfall. The single room was sparsely furnished with what might once have been a table and a chair, which were reduced to splinters and cobwebs. A filthy mattress was shoved into one corner, its springs poking through the fabric like ribs.

Since then, Amari has done a lot of work spread over the years to fix it up. The floorboards have been somewhat restored where she could, and the furniture has been replaced with admittedly cheap products. At least the bed is comfortable enough.

She gently places her backpack on the table—chipped and paint peeling but whole—before finally letting some of the tension leave her body. All she feels in the wake of it is an all-encompassing ache. Her shoulder is the worst by far, and Amari grimaces as she considers her next steps.

Heading over to one corner of the shack, Amari rifles through her bags of personal items—sparse as they are—until she reaches a loose wooden panel on the floor. Lifting it up, she grabs the worn purse stuffed into the hidden space. It's something she lifted off a rare tourist who visited the district, though what it originally contained is long gone.

Inside is a bottle of enchanted medicine.

It's just for simple pain relief, but it's so expensive and highly guarded here that Amari is extremely sparse with how she uses her very meager supply. Only for emergencies, when the pain leftover from her magic leaves her unable to protect herself properly. Similarly, her supply of healing potions is dismal but required in this instance. She applies a salve to her shoulder and wraps it tightly with a wince.

The moment she's done, it's like all her energy exits her at once. Amari briefly considers just lying on the floor where she is, yet bravely makes the agonizing journey to her bed. Being able to rest is such a relief, it brings tears to her eyes, and the thirteen-year-old hastily wipes them away with an embarrassed scowl. She shifts until her horns are no longer digging uncomfortably into the pillow with a sigh.

Instead of focusing on her pain, Amari turns her attention to her surroundings. The shack is familiar but still fascinating in many ways, making it a good enough distraction.

Strange, looping symbols are scrawled across the walls in what appears to be faded chalk—or perhaps something darker. They pulse faintly in the dim light, their meanings long forgotten. Any attempt to erase or cover them results in their reappearance the next time the shack shifts back into existence.

The shack hums with an otherworldly energy, subtle yet impossible to ignore. At night, faint whispers echo through the space, rising and falling in incomprehensible patterns, as though a conversation is being held. Of course, Amari knows that the noise is entirely telepathic projections since she can block them out with strong mental shielding. Objects occasionally move on their own—a battered tin cup sliding across the floor or a warped plank snapping into place when no one is looking. The temperature fluctuates wildly, sometimes plunging into an icy chill, other times becoming oppressively hot.

Sometimes, the ghost manifests itself: a faint figure with indistinct features flickering like a damaged projection. It doesn't appear malicious but seems curious, lingering in corners or watching the shack's occupant with faint, glowing eyes. On rare occasions, it moves objects to "help"—a plank repositioning itself to create a makeshift step or a dropped item mysteriously appearing back on the mattress.

It's... comforting, not to be completely alone. Amari is self-aware enough to know that's weird, except she can't bring herself to care very much.

Soon, her eyelids get heavier and heavier, the exhaustion of the day hitting her like a train. She's so tired that most of her sleep is dreamless.

But not entirely.

When it began, Amari was turning the kettle on and putting a tea bag in a mug. She heard the howling of the wind and the rattling of the door. With a home so high in the mountains, this tripped no alarms for her. She didn't fear anything until the screams started.

A part of Amari recognized this as a dream because it was a memory. This was the end, she remembered—the end of the seers.

Outside, the wind picked up, and the house shook under its rage. The door banged open, and Amari got a glimpse of the chaos outside.

A storm made of fire ripped through everything. It was terrible. It already happened.

Amari distantly realized she dropped her mug on the floor. Shattered ceramic covers the tile. Her slippers carelessly walked through it as she ran to the door. On the threshold, she saw the end of the seers.

A community of people with foresight—they knew their end was near. It didn't save them.

The house's foundations shook all around her, and parts of the roof were torn away. People tried to run, or pray, or fight.

Amari will survive this. She will be the only one to. This doesn't make the dream any easier.

The screams seemed unending. It took her a moment to realize the screeching was from the kettle. She hadn't noticed that the pressure had built up to that point. Amari had the insane urge to scream with it. To throw something or tear something apart.

Her dreamscape shifted around her, changing from her house to a bird's-eye view of Castor. Amari had a split second to adjust before an explosion took out a portion of the Lower District. Fire spread, engulfing what remained.

"No!" She shouted.

Not again. Never again.

The kettle's whistle still echoed in her ears as everything went dark.

Amari jolts awake with such a start that she falls off her bed and onto the floor. The shock of hitting the wood and the sudden cold ground her in reality as she grapples with the aftereffects of the dream. Getting a vision, whether in sleep or awake, always leaves her questioning the world around her.

The ache in her shoulder—dulled by the pain medication and the healing salve—is a good grounding device even as she grimaces. She moves to sit up and finds her water bottle politely put down right next to her. It makes her realize how thirsty she is, and Amari whispers a thanks before nearly drowning herself in her haste to drink.

As soon as her head is on right, she reaches under her bed and pulls a notebook from a hidden nook in the frame. A pen is tied to it, and she opens the book with practiced ease. Amari uses a sharp nail to flip to the first blank page she finds and begins writing her recollection of the vision immediately, not wanting to forget a single bit until it's written down. Having a physical record of her seer abilities is a great risk, considering her status as an illegal being. She would be hunted down and executed by the Apolon Empire if word ever got out. But to Amari, letting such important details be forgotten is even worse.

The routine is a comfort at least, and approaching the matter more scientifically makes it easier for Amari to divorce herself from the feelings the vision provoked. She already spends enough time reliving the end of the seers.

Once the hurried note-taking is finished, Amari is hit with how tired she is all over again. A few hours of restless sleep wasn't enough, so she drags herself back into her bed with a small amount of dread. Thankfully, visions tend to be spaced out, so she shouldn't get two in one night. It's a cold comfort as she lets the exhaustion sweep her away.

It's far into the next day when she finally decides it's time to stop hiding. This is usually when Amari ventures outside since it's still light enough for most humans to be up and about, yet close enough to nightfall that she doesn't have to wait long. Moreover, she's had plenty of time for the healing salve to have a strong impact on her injury. While not completely healed, it is no longer at risk for infection or simply tearing back open.

There are some people she should warn about the Rooftop King, Amari remembers. And she needs to know if the familiar relayed the news of an eavesdropper back to him. Being hunted by the most prominent gang in the district would be... Annoying.

Her vision is also a factor. She has to imagine they're connected since she saw Castor being blown up right after learning something new about the Rooftop King. The urgency that lives under her skin is strong evidence that Amari is right.

She reluctantly exits the shack, squinting in the sunlight and holding back a scowl. Making her way discreetly to the less rundown areas of Castor is a familiar routine, but the added paranoia is a nuisance.

In the daytime, street vendors crowd the narrow walkways, peddling shoddy magical goods from carts barely held together by enchanted nails. Curses in bottles, love spells scratched into crumbling amulets, and glowing potions of questionable origin are hawked to desperate buyers, their sellers gesturing at customers over the general din. Their goods are cheap but dangerous, prone to unintended consequences or fading moments after purchase. Children dart between the carts, their grubby hands quick to swipe loose talismans or glowing trinkets, with angry vendors left in their wake.

Amari stays well clear of them all. Normally, she might even take to the roofs to avoid attention, except that's not really an option now. The thought is enough to sour her mood further.

The criminal underbelly thrives in this magic-scarred district. Sometimes, when they're bold enough, enforcers clad in cobbled-together magical armor patrol the streets. If one pays attention, they might catch shadowy figures whispering incantations under their breath in the corners of dim alleys, summoning small, flickering familiars, or weaving hexes to settle disputes. Occasionally, a burst of uncontrolled magic erupts—a glowing rune accidentally set off, or a back alley duel escalates into fireballs that scorch nearby buildings.

When it comes to the Rooftop King, however, most disputes happen in the air, or at least from a high vantage point. The Sky Lords in his gang can get particularly rowdy and don't really care about hiding it. Amari watches the sky with wary eyes.

She makes her way through winding streets towards storefronts with more polished appearances. Even people with few resources can put effort into their neighborhood to make it look nice. For Amari, it's always comforting to see. She's still used to a more close-knit community. Her childhood home feels at once like a ghost looming over her shoulders and a million miles away into the past.

Her nostalgic mood is killed as she's trailing through an empty side street when her powers deign to inform her that she's being watched. A sharp, shooting awareness hits her right between the eyes. As soon as she notices it, the feeling is oppressive, and Amari nearly freezes on the spot like an amateur. Instead, she keeps walking casually and tries to covertly catch a glimpse of her stalker, to no avail.

Gritting her teeth hard enough for her sharp canines to bite into her lip, the seer strays from the direction she's heading so she can focus on losing her tail. This involves ducking into alleyways, passing through stores, and some minor parkour over low walls. The feeling of being watched doesn't abate, which all but confirms that her stalker is at a high vantage point.

The obvious suspect is an agent of the Rooftop King. Even the thought is enough to make Amari nauseated. Did the gangster already send someone to track her down? How was she found so quickly?

With measured breaths, Amari regains control of her nerves and pushes her worries away. She needs a solution—

or, at least, a plan.

Glancing around, she eyes the streets of Castor idly. All this time, she's stuck to the Lower District in hopes of losing the stalker in the confusing twists and turns of this place. But if her tail is someone the Rooftop King sent, then they're just as familiar with this sector as she is, if not more, for being born here.

So, if losing her stalker is impossible, and confrontation is likely... Amari may as well choose where to make her stand.

Without being obvious, the seer starts making her way back north. To the one watching her, it may look like she's heading back to the abandoned neighborhood she calls home. However, there's a reason very few venture to this area of Castor.

Every part of the city is some measure of haunted. Most scholars agree that the source of this energy is in the northern sector of the Lower District.

The Kiyoshi Crater is a scar set into the foundation of Castor, both literally and figuratively. From above, it looks like a dark stain in the otherwise civilized city. It's technically off-limits, but the boundary around it is easy enough to get past. Most people simply don't want to be near it. Amari isn't overly fond of the place herself, especially since she is more likely to perceive the crater's ambient magic than others.

When her destination becomes clear, she can *feel* the moment her stalker hesitates. Following her into the city's most haunted site is probably a bit intimidating. Will they keep up?

Amari quickly makes her way past the boundary, and the process is somewhat familiar at this point. She's immediately assaulted by senses of time long past. Voices from thousands of years ago are directly projected into her mind, and she catches flickers of scenes out of the corner of her eye. With a wary sigh, she ignores the sensations with practiced ease and avoids the skeletal trees that dot the crater. Plants are given a wide berth since nothing that grows here is meant for humans. The bioluminescent flowers and reaching vines are beautiful in the way many dangerous things are.

As Amari ventures deeper into the crater, she sees a spot in the open where she can camp out. While time to rest is needed after yesterday's hectic events, the seer is more interested in whether her stalker will make a move. Waiting is a boring game, but a necessary one.

It depends, Amari thinks as she plops down onto a flat rock jutting out of the blackened earth, on whether her tail is supposed to only monitor her or if something more nefarious is planned as well. If it's just surveillance, she can use the crater to lose them. However, a confrontation here would mean Amari has the advantage.

It doesn't take long.

A change in the stagnant air of the crater alerts her to the danger as a knife buries itself in the earth by her feet. Startled despite waiting for this very thing, Amari tumbles off the rock. She quickly rights herself, landing on crouched feet and eyes roving the area. There are few places to hide here, yet the assailant manages it.

The shift of a shadow is her only sign of what comes next, and Amari throws herself to the side as a small figure leaps out from the skeletal branches of a tree. How they concealed themself so well is still running in the back of her mind as she tries to gain distance between her attacker.

It doesn't work well when up against the sheer speed of her stalker, who propels themself forward with a single bound and slashes a longer blade at her. Amari narrowly dodges it, feeling the displaced air by her shoulder. Without pause, the attack redirects, and the two find themselves in a deadly dance. Dark clothing conceals most of her stalker, making any identification impossible as Amari tries to keep her head attached to her neck.

In the corner of her mind, she notes the assailant is rather short. Mostly, she's occupied avoiding the blade. Amari briefly considers drawing her own knife but quickly dismisses it. Hers is stashed away in her boot and is a weapon she's not very adept at using, unlike her attacker. Instead, she focuses on using the uneven and unpredictable terrain to her advantage.

Unstable ground, plants neither Amari nor her stalker wants to be near, and flickers of wild magic manifesting are all weaponized. Amari dances closer to the bushes with ominous thorns and mysterious floating lights than most people are ever comfortable approaching. She grabs onto the branches of skeletal trees to launch herself over boulders or foliage and jumps across puddles of liquid that reflect nothing.

To her irritation, her attacker is more fearless than she would like. They follow Amari across the crater with little hesitation, only hindered by their unfamiliarity with the terrain. The seer is fast growing fed-up with it.

Suddenly, her instincts flare at her, nearly making her stumble mid-run. The taste of foreign magic in the air warns her the stalker is doing something, and Amari begins to feel she's moving sluggishly. Her footing feels less certain, and her body is stiff in an unnatural way.

It's not time magic, she knows instantly. For a moment, all she can feel is disappointment before logic kicks back in. This is bad.

With great reluctance, Amari dips into *real* time magic so she can give herself an edge as the attacker catches up. She tries to replicate the feeling of what she did yesterday—

holding Time in her hands—and grits her teeth as her powers slip out of her mental grip like sand through her fingers.

Warning spikes in her mind again, and the feel of a blade skims her back as she throws herself forward into a roll, stumbling clumsily out of it on unsure legs. Again, she tries to control the flow of time around her and fails utterly as she runs on sluggish limbs.

All at once, her body stiffens to the point of freezing, causing her to trip and fall to the ground. Instead of panicking, Amari focuses entirely on Time. The nonlinear lattice of it that lies around her like rolling hills, constant and eternal. For a moment, she can see the tapestry in front of her. Desperately, Amari reaches out and *grabs*.

Something shifts, just slightly.

The flash of light reflecting off a blade brings her back to the Present, and Amari dodges the slowed-down attack just in time. While her attacker is still under the effects of her power, she takes off toward a jagged crack in the crater that oozes malevolent energy. Whatever magic is making her body sluggish is lessened against her power.

She leaps across the crack without hesitation, timing it just right so a blast of hot air coming from it sends her meters upward. The momentum launches her the rest of the way across the crack. Amari lands without any grace to speak of but with no broken bones. Her shoulder aches something fierce, though.

Flames spurt up out of the crack next, stopping her quickly pursuing stalker from following.

They both stop moving without any discussion about it, staring each other down from across the broken earth as fire crackles between them. A swarm of soft, floating lights spins around them, high above and largely harmless from Amari's experience. The small phenomena are a lesser manifestation of will-o'-wisps, congregating around places like the Kiyoshi Crater. However, her attacker shouldn't know that. They're remarkably and annoyingly unbothered.

At least now the seer can finally stop and get a good look at the stalker. She's expecting a Sky Lord ruffian like the ones at the docks, or something similar. That's not what she finds.

To her shock, the figure standing fearlessly in Kiyoshi Crater doesn't look any older than her. Amari actually freezes for a moment, taken aback by the other child glaring at her. Her stalker's gender isn't immediately clear, since a well-wrapped scarf is pulled up to cover the lower half of their face. From what she can see, they have dark skin, black hair twisted into a tight braid, and yellow eyes narrowed in her direction.

Something in the girl's posture changes, and Amari belatedly recognizes she's being spoken to. Of course, with the other's mouth covered, she scowls in response.

"Uh. I'm deaf," Amari says, feeling strangely awkward about revealing information that should be objectively alarming. But she'd rather attempt to have a productive conversation than try to guess at what the other is saying. "I have some paper in my bag—"

She's cut off by the other raising her hands, making Amari tense instinctively for some kind of attack. Instead, the girl starts making motions with her hands, which Amari quickly recognizes.

"How did you know I was there?" The question is asked in sign language, the hand movements holding a sense of ease to them that show a high level of familiarity. Something in Amari loosens even as the situation remains tense.

"A bad feeling," she answers, giving a partial truth. It's close enough without being revealing, and she can't exactly give a better reason when she failed to spot her stalker even once. The girl's brow furrows in what looks like irritation, making Amari sure she's scowling under the scarf.

"You're weird," the girl signs, pointing emphatically on the *you*. Against her better judgment, Amari rolls her eyes.

"Says the stalker."

"Assassin," the *assassin* spells out, nonplussed by her divulging this information far too casually. The flames start to die down, and Amari tenses. "You pissed off the Rooftop King. Why?"

"You don't know?" Amari questions as she grapples with the fact that the gangster instantly jumped to the most extreme option. What did he think she overheard? Not being able to hear the Sky Lords yesterday is looking more and more like a regret. Being Deaf and all.

"I'm just a hired hand," the girl waves off with an unfazed air. Yellow eyes train on her with an intensity that stills the seer. "But now I'm curious."

So this assassin isn't a part of the Rooftop King's gang? What does that mean? Amari studies the other, trying to read her intentions.

Reluctantly, Amari reaches out mentally to her magic, ignoring the sharp shooting pain it creates behind her eyes. She's still not recovered enough to be doing this so flagrantly, but needs must. The familiar feeling of possibilities lying like a map around her greets the seer, but the warning of danger doesn't appear. Despite the very real assassin in front of her, none of Amari's instincts are going off now that knives are no longer being tossed around.

... Maybe her seer powers are broken.

She's finally done it somehow. The first seer—the *last* seer—to break their powers! Great. Just what she needs right now.

"He thinks I overheard something yesterday," Amari elects

to reveal, holding back a grimace. The assassin's shoulder shakes like she's laughing, and her hands quickly snap a few choice words insulting the gangster's intelligence. It's enough to make the seer's mouth twitch into a small smile. "You seem like you're no longer trying to kill me."

The other girl shrugs. "I'm debating whether it's worth the money I was paid."

"What would help convince you it's not?" Amari hedges, seeing a chance to escape this situation without violence. The flames are all but gone entirely, yet she's no longer preparing to run.

Her stalker taps their chin with glove-covered fingers before shaping an answer. "You don't know what information the Rooftop King wants to be silenced at all?"

Answering a question with a question. Amari argues with herself about how much to divulge on a hunch before steeling her resolve. "I was in the Upper District, hiding in the docks. I saw two of his minions talking with a merchant. He was scared of them."

Eyebrows jumping up, the assassin leans back on the soles of her feet as she takes in this information. "Wow. Someone's expanding. And keeping it a secret..."

"You don't like the Rooftop King." It's not a question. Amari bets on her instincts and watches carefully for the other's reaction.

Surprisingly—or maybe not surprisingly from everything she's seen with this girl—the assassin instantly nods in agreement. She starts to sign with exaggerated movements for emphasis. "All that man does is bully people and act like he really is a king. I've only remained a freelancer because his influence is limited to the Lower District, and I work throughout all of Castor."

"Then this is bad news for you," Amari pounces on the

knowledge, mindful of not coming off as too enthusiastic. She's sure the other is scowling again. "Something needs to be done."

The assassin leans forward, eyes locked on hers. "Are you offering?"

Amari stills, her own words catching up to her. *Is she offering to help? What is she saying?* "That's..."

"Because if you are," the other signs with smooth motions, eyes unblinking. "I have an idea."

"You assume I want to work with someone who's been hired to kill me."

To her irritation, the assassin waves this concern away like it's nothing. "If I were being serious, you would already be dead. I was following you out of curiosity more than anything once you noticed my presence."

Amari can't suppress her scowl at the words and sees the other laugh in response. "What plan is this? You can't really expect two kids to take on a gangster, can you?"

"Not in a fight, maybe," hands pause to reach up and pull down the scarf. A sharp grin greets Amari. "But I'm Taliya Camry, the best assassin and thief in Castor. And you are...?"

The seer sighs, debating again whether or not to trust her gut before forging on. Her instincts are basically all she has at this point. "Amari. No one special."

"You've managed to gain a lot of attention for someone so ordinary," Taliya needles, mockery clear from her gestures.

"Call me unlucky," Amari deadpans, resisting the desire to scoff. "Now, the plan?"

"More of an idea than a plan."

"Of course it is."

Amari is still questioning how she got into this situation as she and Taliya stake out the Rooftop King's headquarters. They had left the Kiyoshi Crater quickly, as it's not a place to linger long, and discussed the other girl's idea at length as they walked the winding streets. To be fair, it's not a bad idea at all. It's just in dire need of an actual plan to go along with it.

The stakeout is technically Amari's proposal since she refused to take any action without information about the Rooftop King. That doesn't make actually carrying it out any less nerve-wracking.

Next to her, Taliya is lying upside down and picking at her nails with the dagger she threw at Amari. The assassin soon grew bored of just sitting and watching, barely avoiding giving their spot away with her dramatics.

"How are you an assassin and a thief if you have no patience for anything?"

Reading sign language upside down is significantly more difficult, and it takes an extra moment for her to parse as Taliya waves her hands about.

"I usually have an exciting end goal! Just watching to get information is *so* boring! What am I supposed to prepare for?"

"Knowledge."

Taliya sends her a rude gesture. The seer smirks and turns her eyes back to the Rooftop King's home.

The actual headquarters is too large to spy on all at once. It's a fortress hidden in plain sight, perched high above the bustling city and cloaked in shadow. Known as the Spirehaven, it is an intricate, labyrinthine network of rooftops, bridges, and concealed chambers that crown the city's skyline. Accessible only through risky climbs, secret pathways, and leaps across precarious ledges, the Spirehaven is both a refuge and a stronghold.

Amari is still surprised by the size of the headquarters spread across the interconnected rooftops of several abandoned buildings in the city's older district. Weathered slate tiles and crumbling chimneys blend seamlessly into the skyline, making the Spirehaven nearly invisible from the streets below. Ivy and moss cling to the structures, adding to the illusion of decay, but closer inspection reveals carefully maintained platforms, reinforced beams, and trapdoors hidden beneath layers of grime.

The gang is largely made up of Sky Lords, and their base is actively hard to reach for anyone who can't fly. Wooden bridges and tightrope-thin walkways connect the rooftops, forming a dizzying maze of pathways that only the Rooftop King's trusted operatives, or daring fools like her and Taliya, can navigate with ease. The assassin told Amari that some of these connections are booby-trapped, with loose planks, collapsing ropes, or magical wards designed to repel intruders. Others require skilled parkour to traverse, with gaps so wide and drops so deadly that only the fearless—or the desperate—attempt the journey.

Set up out of sight on a roof across, Amari and Taliya spy on the headquarters' central hub. Located at the heart of the Spirehaven is the King's Court, a rooftop plaza sheltered beneath a massive, slanted canopy of stitched-together tarps and weathered sails. This canopy provides cover from the elements while leaving the space open to the ever-changing sky. Strings of dim, flickering lanterns hang above, casting the area in a warm yet eerie glow, their light dancing across the cracked tiles and weathered timbers.

The court is a hive of activity. Operatives—pickpockets, spies, messengers, and enforcers—gather here to report to their lieutenants, trade stolen goods, or share news from the city below. Makeshift tables and crates serve as meeting spaces, while a handful of covered alcoves offer privacy for more sensitive dealings. The faint hum of magic lingers in the air, woven into wards that alert the King's followers to intruders or danger.

Amari and Taliya have managed to avoid detection because of the assassin's talent with wardbreaking and familiarity with the court's defenses. Apparently, being an assassin and a thief requires one to be a skillful Scribe— someone who can write and nullify runes. Taliya wields her runica with such ease as she draws her own wards that it makes Amari feel a curl of envy.

The seer has some traditional training in scribework, but she is woefully unprepared for the illegal activities she finds herself partaking in. And the lack of classical education seems to be working in Taliya's favor as she casually breaks and remakes the laws of runes. Sometimes, Amari realizes, rules are more troublesome than helpful.

In the court, she watches the perch of inactive familiars uneasily. A host of the same kind of creature that attacked her at the docks, all identical.

Familiars are intelligent and fiercely loyal to their master, operating with a cold, calculating efficiency. They rarely show emotions, are only driven by their created purpose, and carry out commands without hesitation. However, some do exhibit more animal-like behavior. The ones the Rooftop King uses are rumored to have a sense of superiority, often toying with their prey before delivering the final blow or darting just out of reach to frustrate attackers.

According to Taliya, these creatures are both a symbol of the gang leader's power and an extension of his influence. The familiar's presence at a meeting or deal sends an unspoken message: the Rooftop King is always watching, constantly aware. Those who see the faint glow of its eyes in the shadows know better than to act against their master, for the familiar's retribution is swift and precise.

The creature's ability to spy, relay information, and neutralize threats makes it indispensable for maintaining the gang's dominance in the Lower District. And Amari fought one and survived. No wonder she had an assassin trailing her the next day. She's lucky Taliya is so free-spirited and self-serving.

Something in this court suddenly catches her eye. In the throng of gangsters and shady denizens is a well-dressed man leaving the room, sometimes referred to as the Rooftop King's 'throne room.' Neither Amari nor Taliya calls it that.

The man has the characteristic tall, twisted horns and commonly red hair of a Sun Eater. Despite the nicely tailored clothes, he's rather tall and looks like he can hold his own in a fight. Someone tough, but who cares about appearances. "Hey, who's that?"

Taliya leans forward with an annoying lack of urgency and squints in the direction Amari is pointing. It's clear the assassin's eyesight is not quite as good as hers. "Oh. That's the docks foreman for the Lower District. He's been living in the Rooftop King's pocket for years."

"And they'll no doubt need his help to branch out to the other districts," Amari says, and Taliya nods along. "Okay, let's follow him when we leave."

"*Yes,*" Taliya gestures enthusiastically. She all but springs to her feet when the man they're watching leaves the court, escorted by a Sky Lord who takes the foreman down from the rooftops. He's deposited off a main street where no one is looking (that they know of) and swiftly left alone to go home. Since night is setting in and the foreman is not a Nightblood, she's confident in her deduction that he's done working for the day.

Castor's Lower District doesn't have a wealthy neighborhood, but the outskirts, farthest from Kiyoshi Crater, *are* more put together than most buildings here. Impressively, the paint barely peels, and the plants don't overrun the place. Amari imagines it's someone's full-time job to combat the effects the ambient magic here has.

This is unsurprisingly where the foreman lives, paying for his nicely kept house with money from the Rooftop King, no doubt. Amari wonders how many smuggled goods pass under his watch every day. It must be a lucrative business with the Merchant District next door.

"Alright, we meet back in the morning," Amari says, hoping her voice is firm. Trying to snoop in the foreman's house when the man is still there is foolish. Taliya hardly needs such things explained to her, the experienced thief that she is, and agrees easily.

They depart without a word, and Amari goes back to her little dilapidated shack to collapse into her bed. Exhaustion catching up with her, she has a pleasant, dreamless sleep.

Morning starts early and quietly, Amari struggling out of her covers and into something suited for a break-in. Not that she has an outfit specifically for such things. What would that even look like? A cat-suit, or something tactical like that?

She makes do with cheap clothes that won't get caught if she's climbing. The seer anxiously fiddles with her ram horns, wondering if they could potentially get in the way before banishing the worry to the depths of her mind. Amari should be more concerned about her markings being seen. Maybe Taliya will let her borrow that scarf...

The trip to the foreman's home is nerve-wracking, and she doubts herself every other turn she takes, making the journey unnecessarily long. Taliya is waiting in a side street by the time she arrives.

"Sun's already up," the assassin points out with agitated hands. Amari fights the urge to physically wilt, scolding herself for the absurd thought.

"Did you see the foreman leave?"

"Yeah."

"Then we're doing this," Amari says, hopefully sounding more certain than she feels. The other doesn't continue complaining, so it must work to a degree.

"Um, can—" the seer starts, then stops awkwardly and winces. Unfortunately, Taliya clearly hears her cut-off remark and looks at her curiously. Amari decides to dive onward regardless of the discomfort stirring in her chest. "Can I use your scarf to hide my markings? I know it doesn't cover the crescent moon on the side of my forehead or the other markings higher up, but—"

Taliya shrugs and lazily signs a *yes*. It brings a surge of instant relief with it, even as part of Amari's mind is apprehensive of the quick agreement. Without any fuss, the thief uncoils the dark scarf from her neck and passes it to the seer.

"You know how to put it on?" Taliya's hands hold a question as an eyebrow is raised in question. Amari grimaces slightly as she holds the scarf. She didn't know how to ensure the soft material covered her face and stayed there during a break-in. Hesitantly, she shakes her head.

Taliya reaches forward and grabs the scarf. For a moment, Amari thinks the assassin is taking it back, but instead, she starts winding it around the seer's neck gently. The closeness of another human after years without is startling, and Amari freezes as the other carefully fixes the cloth in place. Taliya pulls a piece over her face, resting securely over the bridge of her nose. It easily conceals most of her markings, and the prospect of that safety is more satisfying than she realized it would be.

"Ready?" Taliya asks with a fast motion, a smirk playing on her lips as she steps back out of Amari's personal space. The seer takes a moment to center herself and reach out cautiously to her magic. Nothing alarming waits around the corner that she can sense.

"Ready," Amari says.

Together, they approach the backside of the foreman's house.

It's a nice two-story structure, the walls crafted from smooth gray stone interspersed with warm wooden accents. The stonework has been enchanted to glisten faintly in the sunlight, giving it a polished, almost pearlescent sheen. Such a cosmetic use of magic makes Amari wrinkle her nose. Who's wasting energy reactivating that every month or so?

The roof, made of sleek slate tiles designed to repel dirt and rain, neatly frames the structure. Even from the back, it's meant to be stylish. In the backyard, a small but meticulously maintained garden surrounds the house, filled with pointless but pretty plants—nothing that could be used for food or medicine. A winding stone path, embedded with small runestones that Taliya had inspected before dismissing, leads them to the back porch, where a charming wooden bench and a hanging lantern complete the scene.

On the back door are intricate carvings of protective glyphs that glow softly when approached, welcoming invited guests while quietly deterring ill-intentioned visitors. Taliya eyes them dispassionately with the air of someone who's often seen this type of thing. Amari watches in fascination as the thief pulls out her runica—a sleek black pen-like device that channels one's magic into writing or, in this case, *breaking* runes.

Unfortunately, Amari isn't well-versed enough to

understand what Taliya is doing once she starts wardbreaking, and her eyes wander. The house's tall, arched windows are framed with dark wood and seem to have plenty of enchantments. It's all very dull as she waits to get into the building.

Once inside, Amari is immediately assaulted by the foreman's idea of art. The pieces aren't *bad*, per se, but she gets the impression the foreman is trying to portray an image of wealth he doesn't have. In one painting, two dragons, one made of fire and the other of lightning, are locked in an eternal, animated battle. The flames and lightning flicker vividly, casting harsh, clashing colors across the hallway. Their movements are overly dramatic and repetitive, creating a chaotic sense of motion that never quite feels harmonious. Another piece of art depicts a massive stag with golden antlers that gleam so intensely they dominate the painting. In the same hallway, they clash terribly.

It feels so needlessly gaudy that she avoids looking at them. Even her experiments with bright colored paints as a small child didn't result in travesties like this.

She barely manages to move past her disgust as Taliya scans the hall with a well-trained eye. Amari follows the thief through the floorspace, taking note of all the places she stops to search for any wards—mostly in doorways, windows, and shelves.

"The office?" Amari signs to Taliya, some instinct in her telling her not to make any noise, even if the house is empty.

The thief points upward, indicating the upper floor. They creep up the stairs slowly as Taliya keeps alert for any traps. It's unlikely for the foreman to be so paranoid, Amari figures, but the other girl would know better than her the kind of security richer folk have.

Upstairs, the artwork that sprinkles the walls doesn't

improve. She wrinkles her nose and elects to ignore the decorations entirely as Taliya leads her past a couple of doors. Each entryway is inspected and then discarded until the thief reaches one that gives her pause. Amari is all but dying from curiosity about the criteria.

Taliya has her runica out and wardbreaking the next moment, the seer peering at her work with fascination. This process takes longer than the wards outside did, and Amari's eyes widen. Was Taliya looking for the most warded spot in the house? That makes sense.

As if to confirm her theory, the door swings open to reveal a neat-looking office. The artwork is worse here, depicting a sorcerer in gold robes, with a smug expression, surrounded by glowing, floating orbs of light. The sorcerer winks at them as they walk in, which Amari feels is deeply unnerving rather than impressive magic work.

Otherwise, the office is rather sparse, and Amari imagines it's mainly used as a status symbol. The foreman undoubtedly has another office he uses more where he works. His desk seems well-crafted, the wood shining in the morning light.

Taliya wastes no time gawking. As soon as the door opens, the thief tracks down any remaining wards in the room to dismantle, then begins going through every single thing. It's almost alarming how fast Taliya rifles through drawers and shelves.

Hastily, Amari joins her and decides to focus on the desk. It takes her a moment to read the print on the documents she finds because her Esmesian is usually limited to reading store windows or books with a more straightforward style of writing. The legal speak in the documents makes her squint as she takes it in and sorts it through her mind to make sense of it. If nothing else, this adventure has taught her that she has little interest in being a lawyer.

Though learning to speak the language of the wealthy and resourceful has its merits...

Taliya pulls Amari from her train of thought when the thief swings open the gaudy painting to reveal a safe in the wall. Taliya turns to Amari, hands emphasizing the thief's smirk and movements, adding to the overall smugness. "Classic."

Her frame shaking with soft laughter, Amari briefly abandons the desk to inspect the safe. To her novice eyes, it looks rather secure, but the thief next to her seems unworried and amused.

More tools than just the runica come out for this next bit, as Taliya puts something between the safe and her ear. In addition, she's thematically running her glove-covered fingers around the rim of the lock. Why, Amari has no idea and feels awkward asking about.

A moment later, her accomplice grins brightly and opens the unlocked safe with a triumphant swing. Inside lies a large stack of files.

Taliya's smile instantly drops. "Boring," she over-enunciates, then signs for further emphasis so Amari knows exactly why she's disappointed. The seer rolls her eyes and walks forward.

"This is good," Amari responds lightly, hoping none of her amusement at the other's disdain is leaking into her voice. The look on the thief's face tells her she's not very successful. Mouth twitching, she carefully takes the stack of documents, knowing as she picks it up that they don't have time to search through it here. "We came here for information. It must be important if it was in there."

Waving her hands dismissively, Taliya closes the safe and painting with a pout. "Guess we're going to have to look through all that, huh?"

"Not here," Amari states the obvious. She bites her lip a

second later as she balances the stack of files in her arms. "Do you, uh, know a safe place where we can work?"

Taliya doesn't blink at the request, simply tilting her head back in thought. Her golden eyes stare a hole into the ceiling as she goes over places. Amari wonders if the other is debating whether or not she can trust the seer with knowing —

"Yeah, I hang around a cool safehouse by the river, sometimes."

Amari blinks, watching the thief blankly for a moment. Then she asks stupidly, "And you'll take me there?"

"It's not super moldy, promise." Taliya's movements are sharp, like she needs to convince Amari of this. The seer squints with visible apprehension. "Really. It's got a nice view!"

"That's not what... Nevermind, we're wasting time. Show me the way."

Taliya's face notably brightens before turning back to focused seriousness. "Files in the bag, first. Can't be running around with that in the open."

She holds out her bag—a rather bland satchel with a cross-strap and some pins of comically drawn cats on it—for Amari to place the stack in. The seer stares at the small bag, then the large pile of documents, and back to the bag. Her looks are pointed enough for Taliya to catch onto her concern.

"Oh! Right, you're a newbie. Here, see?" Taliya then sticks her *entire arm* into the bag up to her shoulder despite there being no visible room.

"A *dimensional pocket?*" Amari questions, probably too loudly. "How the—"

The thief shushes her, and she winces as she dials her voice down. Amari asks more calmly this time. "How can you afford that?"

"Stole it."

Of course.

After that minor confusion, Amari dumps the stack of files in Taliya's bag without hesitation and gapes in wonder over how even the weight remains unchanged.

"How much can fit in there?"

"A lot," the thief says smugly. "But you gotta be mindful. Trying to go over the limits of enchantments—especially ones that affect reality—usually leads to bad results. So, you know, don't try to use this bag to smuggle out a couch or something."

Leaving the foreman's house is much easier than breaking into it. According to Taliya, this is because there's little point in pretending they didn't break in since they took everything from the safe.

"We'll need to go through each file today," Amari states firmly, mind running over anything and everything that could go wrong. "They'll know someone's after them now, so the information we find—"

"Let's just find out when we get there!" Taliya signs casually as she leads Amari through the streets. They end up by the riverbank rather quickly, where the general appearance of the Lower District seems nicer to those arriving in Castor. Fewer dilapidated houses and broken roads where tourists can plainly see. Taliya stops at a random apartment building, motioning the seer inside.

"Seriously?"

Nodding with an easy smile playing on her face, the thief leads her up the stairs to the top floor. Taliya picks a lock on one of the apartment doors with a speed that suggests familiarity, even for an accomplished burglar. Amari narrows her eyes as she takes in the living space she's been taken to.

The apartment is nothing fancy, except it's such a step up from her little haunted shack that she's not sure what to do for a moment. Her next thought is that no one lives here.

The apartment feels more like a waiting room than a home—bare walls, unscuffed floors, and not a single personal touch to suggest who, if anyone, truly lives here. A faint shimmer lingers in the air, as if the space itself remembers spells once cast, though no magic actively hums against Amari's skin. Windows offer a view of the river below, its surface reflecting shifting light like a living mirror, but inside, the apartment remains untouched—just empty space, holding its breath.

Taliya drops the bag on a table against a wall and opens the window next to it with an air of routine. The view of the river is beautiful, and Amari imagines this place must be expensive to rent.

"How do you know about this place?"

"Oh," Taliya rubs the back of her neck sheepishly before lifting her hands. "I know the owner, that's all!"

Amari keeps her eyes trained on Taliya, waiting for a more honest answer. She says nothing, well aware that the black sclera and white irises of a Nightblood are plenty unnerving on their own. Just as she predicted, the thief breaks down a few moments later.

"Alright, I might have killed the owner's abusive ex in exchange for letting me use this place occasionally."

That's... "Practical," Amari comments, and sits down at the table. Now Taliya is looking at her intensely for some reason.

"It—yeah. Want some tea?"

The thought of tea is such a relief after the last forty-eight hours that Amari nearly bursts into tears on the spot. It's embarrassing how deeply the memories affect her, even now.

She reasons with herself that she has only managed to have tea a few times since she came to Castor, so the prospect is exciting.

"That would be amazing," she admits. Taliya grins and gets up with what must be endless energy. Amari turns to the window as she waits, taking in the view. She rarely has the spare time for this kind of quiet, as ironic as it is. Between survival and, well, *revenge*, Amari has a lot on her mind.

The river laps gently on the banks, sparkling under the sun in an inviting way that feels entirely disconnected from her last visit to the water. She can vividly remember the cold from being submerged and the docks shaking under the familiar's fury.

A diving bird hunting for fish makes her jolt, and her heart rate is beating fast even as Amari acknowledges the animal is no threat. The sudden movement both sends jitters through her body and reminds her to stay in the present. Always dangerous for a seer to wander far from that. One could get lost.

Taliya waves her arm into Amari's sight line as she re-enters the room, holding one steaming mug and balancing another on her head without any trouble. Amari is too bemused and baffled to be alarmed. She gratefully accepts the tea when it's handed to her and takes a cautious sniff. Her expectations for Castor tea are low, but the flowery yet herbal scent that greets her is pleasant.

The taste is unfamiliar, as well, yet it's good. Tension leaves Amari's frame in increments. She savors every sip, eyelids half-closed as she contemplates the horizon. Despite the peaceful moment, the enormity of what they're doing is hanging over her head constantly.

She glances discreetly at the assassin sitting across from her. Amari still isn't sure what to make of Taliya, who doesn't seem to fit the image of what an assassin *should* be. What made her go down this path? Pure desperation? But why not stay a thief when she is so clearly talented at it?

Skillful Scribes are highly sought after as well, and Taliya's wardbreaking was amazing. Amari remembers little of how to write runes from when she was in school, and it looked like Taliya didn't follow typical conventions at all. That kind of creativity with magic is a real talent.

And runework... Amari sits up straight in her chair, which catches Taliya's attention.

"Can you write body enhancement runes?"

"Uh, yes?"

From what she understands, body enhancement magic is pretty straightforward. Using runes is the simplest way to achieve the results, whether they be increased strength, speed, or their senses, in this case. She could use runes to enhance her hearing.

However, it's highly regulated and used mainly by soldiers. Amari is supposed to use the artifices sold in stores for assistance, but they're too expensive for her to contemplate. And walking around with stolen devices on her head isn't what she considers *discreet.*

Runes, though... Amari could easily hide them with her hair, and if guards were close enough to see them, she would have bigger problems than illegal scribe charges. The enhancements would be a tax on her magic to keep them active, but could be useful.

"Can you teach me how to write hearing enhancement runes?" Amari doesn't like giving a stranger leverage over her, but she still has no bad feelings about this assassin. It's weird, yet comforting.

"Oh, yeah. I can!" Taliya seems to get excited at the prospect, smiling as her hands move fast. She grabs a piece of scrap paper and a pen from her bag, quickly sketching out the correct runes. "These are what you're looking for, but you need to be careful how much energy you channel into them. Too much of any sense can be overwhelming, and could hurt your body."

"I'll start small," Amari assures the thief. She has no intention of trying to push her limits. "Can I borrow your runica to try it out?"

Runicas are pretty easy to come by, but the quality of them is another matter. Any runica Amari could afford would be old or poorly made. It just makes sense to see what the runes feel like with a top-tier runica like Taliya's.

"Sure," Taliya is a little more cautious, handing over her prized tool, and Amari is appropriately careful as she takes it.

Pulling her sleeve back, Amari brings the runica down on her arm. Writing it closer to her ears would be better for the magic, but unwise since this is her first time.

Having runes written on her skin is a novel experience. At first, all she feels is the cold stone of the runica. It doesn't hurt, thankfully, not like getting a tattoo might. There's a gentle pull on her magic, and she warily channels a small portion of energy through the runes.

Then there's music.

Oh, not much, but there, in the distance. It takes her a minute to decipher what it is. Someone's strumming a guitar and humming along. The soft strings echo up to the window and swiftly bring tears to Amari's dark eyes.

Abruptly, it feels like too much, and Amari subconsciously scales back the magic channeled into the runes. The noise goes down to a more manageable level, and she focuses on the assassin across from her, who looks slightly panicked.

"Uh," Taliya says, and her voice is deeper than what the seer had imagined. Something altogether smoother and younger. "You okay? Shit, are—"

"It's working," Amari chokes out, and her voice is alien to herself. Different from how she remembers, even taking away the emotional tremor.

The thief continues with her flustered fidgeting as she takes the runica back. Her fingers twirl the tool nervously. "O-oh, um, wow, yeah..."

"Sorry," Amari says, not very sincerely. She does feel kinda bad for making the other so uncomfortable. This is a goal she wasn't sure she would ever reach, or at least not without a lot of work and time to afford the artifices. "Thank you."

"Don't..." Taliya murmurs, eyes downward. "Don't thank me."

"I can do what I want."

"Ha!" Taliya seems to startle herself with her laughter, and something more collected takes over her expression. The other's golden eyes meet Amari's squarely.

Perhaps the strangest part is hearing voices again. Not just because the real thing differs from her imagination, but because it makes her use a long-ignored muscle.

She's long used to speaking and reading Esmesian since living in Castor, but hearing it is a new adjustment.

"You're lucky I learned Esmesian at a young age, or I don't think I would understand what you're saying." As it is, it takes Amari a few seconds to translate in her head what Taliya says next.

"Not your native tongue? What is, Apolona?" Taliya asks curiously.

"Kinda," Amari hedges. "Thank you for the tea. I like the flavor."

"Well, it's the apartment's," Taliya rubs the back of her neck sheepishly. "I prefer boba tea, but this stuff's okay."

"Savage," Amari retorts without thinking and only relaxes when the other laughs. Her sharp, blackened nails tap the mug in an off-beat pattern as she forces herself to calm down.

"You don't like boba tea?"

"It's a monstrosity. And gross."

"It's better than regular tea," Taliya says, smirking at the outraged look on the seer's face.

"You can't be serious."

"I will die on this hill," the thief insists.

Amari can't help the snort of laughter that escapes her. "You have so little ground to stand on, you're drowning in the ocean."

"Impossible. I'm an Osiyi," Taliya says with a smirk. Amari's brow rises in surprise before she manhandles her poker face back.

"You're one of the sea folk?"

"Partly, at least," the thief shrugs. "Not a big deal. Lots of mixed kids like me running around in coastal cities with no clue who their parents are."

"... Ah. Sorry."

"Like I said, it's not a big deal. Plus, I get some cool powers from it," Taliya turns to the river and starts singing softly. It's a simple melody, the words from a language no one can translate. Amari's ears twitch at the sound of a Singer, it having been a long time since she heard magic so intertwined in someone's voice. It sends a shiver down her spine and raises all the hair on the back of her neck.

Singers—or sometimes Sirens—can turn words into enchantments, casting magic in an easier but less permanent way than runework. It's powerful magic, but it can be stopped by silencing the singer.

Taliya's voice is deep and soulful, the ancient language of magic rolling off her tongue easily. In the distance, Amari sees the river ripple unnaturally, little swirls forming in the water. Nothing flashy, except that's not the point.

"Amazing," Amari whispers. Then a realization hits her like a speeding cart. "Blood."

Taliya doesn't smother her flinch in time.

"You controlled my blood! In the crater! That's what was going on," Amari realizes, her tone somewhere between accusing and astonished.

"Yeah," the thief admits reluctantly. "You broke out of it, somehow. I would like to know more about, by the way."

"You first."

Taliya looks down and fiddles with her hands, never one to stay still for long without a clear purpose behind it. The seer's eyes soften.

"That's a pretty advanced ability," Amari says, unsure where she's going with this. "You must have studied a lot."

"... Kinda. Not spent a lot of time in school."

"Neither have I. We make do, don't we?"

Taliya smiles. "Yeah, we do."

Silence lapses between them, except it's not uncomfortable or tense. Amari's eyes fall on the bag, her own fingers twitching with the desire to start working. Across from her, the thief rolls her eyes and smirks.

"Fine, let's get started with the boring shit."

She wastes no time pulling out the stack of files, forcing her hands to be careful instead of hasty in her curiosity. Keeping everything neat, she divides the pile into two and pushes one of them to Taliya, who accepts the workload with an exaggerated sigh.

Unsurprisingly, Amari speed reads through the documents

faster than the other, and mentally takes notes as she does. Most of the papers are full of legal terms and the specifics for shipments. She doesn't know enough about either to read between the lines very well, but that's not what she's looking for. Amari grins when she finds obscure mentions of the Upper District's docks.

"The GJS Guild leader is mentioned a lot," Taliya comments idly, flipping through a file lazily. Tilting her head, Amari looks up at her with a clear question on her face. "One of the top merchant guilds here. They're supposed to stick to their own district."

"Ah," Amari says, thinking this information over. The Merchant District has always been a bit of a wildcard. Her own recent venture there makes her reluctant to consider the place. "Taking bribes?"

Taliya shrugs. "Yeah, probably."

A thought scratches at Amari's mind like a pet left stranded outside its home. "What is the GJS guild leader's position with other guild leaders?"

"Uh..." The assassin leans back in her chair, effortlessly balancing on one leg of the furniture. "Not great, I think? There's not been a full war between guilds in a while, but they'll hire hits and stuff from each other's people or assets all the time."

"So this could be a team-up between two groups that want to take over Castor," Amari murmurs, finger tapping her chin thoughtfully. "We should get this information to one of the guild leaders' rivals. It'll leave the Rooftop King without a sponsor and the wind taken out of his sails."

"And distract him from the problem of a random eavesdropper," Taliya smirks as she rights her chair with a thump. "I mean, if I can't find you, who can? You wouldn't be worth the trouble."

"Yeah, that too," the seer says.

Leaving a package of secret files outside a rival guild leader's door and hoping for the best seems wildly unwise, so Amari has to think over methods of delivering information for hours more. No one is likely to put much stock in the words of a street kid, even with physical proof, but they need to strike fast. It's Taliya who points them in the right direction by mentioning that all guild leaders would have informants in each other's places.

"I know a neutral informant here who could get this spread around for a price," the thief suggests.

"Who?"

"You heard of Mia Leon? She's a Nightblood that lives close by and refuses to be affiliated with any one group," Taliya explains, eyes lighting up with renewed energy. "She's real good at what she does and pretty professional. Takes no shit, too."

"Sounds perfect," Amari says, a small smile of relief working its way onto her face. "What kind of payment would she ask for? I'm not exactly swimming in cash."

"Favors, or maybe more information if we can't pay with money. What will cost us is that we're asking her to put herself in danger to spread this information."

"I can handle owing a favor," Amari decides after some thought. "Not sure what other knowledge I can offer, but we'll see when we speak to her."

"Awesome!" Taliya all but springs to her feet. She's been getting up periodically to cartwheel around or do something equally active when sitting too long, yet is still raring to go. Squinting at her from eyes with dark bags attached, Amari sighs. "Let's go!"

"First, we need to make a copy of these files. You know the runes for that, right?"

"Ugh, I do. *Fine.*"

Twenty minutes later, Amari is following Taliya out of the apartment building with a steel resolve in her spine. She's decided to have this problem done today, or at least have a solid plan, so she can go back to her normal existence without all the extra excitement.

Amari doesn't know why the thought feels so disheartening.

Naturally, the two kids have barely started their journey when they run into trouble. Amari knew this day had been going too well.

It starts, as most trouble does, with the seer getting a bad feeling she can't parse. Her powers would be so much more helpful if they could be *concise.* Instead, she's left with last-second instincts, vague feelings, and trying to understand the symbolism of her nightmares.

In the present, Amari is struck by one of her vague bad feelings as she walks with Taliya to meet the informant, Mia. They've left the riverbank behind to head into the more densely populated sector of Castor's Lower District. Since it's the middle of the day, they can easily blend in with the crowds of people going about their lives. The streets are busy as they pass the local food markets and shops. Little golems work as assistants and scurry around in a vain attempt to keep the roads clean.

Nothing seems out of place, yet her bad feeling persists. It makes Amari antsy, with her hands fidgeting with the hem of her jacket and her eyes darting all over the place. Her paranoia turns up nothing, and she forces herself to relax just a bit. Maybe her anxiety is acting up.

She wants to focus on her first time being able to hear everything in Castor. Stepping outside the apartment had been overwhelming, and now she's being bombarded by sounds from all sides. She's already pulled back more of her magic, until most of the background noise is muffled.

The sudden barrage had caused the beginning symptoms of a migraine, so Amari quickly decided to be more frugal with her use of the runes. As they walk, she experiments with how little magic she can use and still pick up that Taliya is whistling next to her.

However, this doesn't mean she's not still alert. Out of all of humanity, Nightbloods have the most extraordinary eyesight—apart from some of the deep-sea Osiyi. Her eyes catch the light flashing off an arrowhead on a roof a kilometer away, and Amari instinctively grabs Taliya as she drops to the ground.

An enchanted arrow whizzes above, just where her head had been. She barely has a moment to question how assassins keep finding her when Taliya pops back to her feet and pulls her into an alleyway. People have started running for cover on the streets, though with much less alarm than would be found in any other part of the city. No one bothers to yell for the guards. An attack from above is the Rooftop King's calling card.

"How were we found?" Amari asks with an aggrieved tone. Surprisingly, she doesn't suspect Taliya of double-crossing her for more than a second before dismissing the possibility entirely.

"I found you," Taliya points out, rather unfazed by the attack. The seer wonders if she deals with other assassins often. "You have to admit, Amari, that there's not a lot of other Nightbloods walking around this time of day."

Amari lets out an angry hiss, seething at herself before focusing back on the situation. "We need higher ground."

Taliya swiftly starts scaling the closest wall to the roof

without hesitation. The ease with which she does it reveals this as her usual method of travel. Amari follows with less sure movements but is no less skilled at climbing. Castor's love of brick-and-mortar buildings with dramatic embellishments makes the task easier.

On the roof, her eyes go to where she initially caught the flash of the arrowhead, only to see an empty space where the assassin would be. "Do you think they'll pursue?"

"I definitely would," Taliya says, hands on her hips. "That arrow was Black Jay's work. She's an assassin who is directly under the Rooftop King."

"Guess he learned his lesson with freelancers," Amari comments dryly, earning a side-eye from the thief.

"Yeah, but the important bit is that she's usually not alone."

Ah.

A sharp shooting of warning hits Amari, and she looks up in time to see something dive-bombing them. "Watch out!"

Amari throws herself to the side as something sickeningly recognizable lands talon-first where she had just been standing. The dragon-like familiar snaps its jaws at her, spiked tail swinging sharply in agitation, and a *second* familiar circles from above. *This is... not good.*

"Shit," Taliya says from a few meters away, having also gotten some distance.

The rooftop bursts into motion, and the girls split up so neither is ganged up against both familiars. This means Amari still has to deal with one alone. Again. She dashes across loose tiles and worn brick with trepidation. Her magic is all over the place, so she relies on experience to outmaneuver the creature.

Amari uses every obstacle—chimneys, abandoned debris, and more—she can find to put between her and the fanged beast. It works out well enough until she turns and runs up to a gap between roofs too wide for her jump.

A sharp screech alerts her to the need to duck and roll, feeling the brush of talons against her hair as she moves. The seer dodges a snap of the familiar's jaws, her mind racing for a solution.

That's when she spots a nearby roof access and gets an idea. Amari keeps running for her life, but now she's looking for Taliya as well, as she turns back.

"Hey!" Amari yells out as soon as she spots Taliya throwing a knife at the other familiar. It bounces off the thing's scales harmlessly yet distracts it enough to let the thief make her way over.

"Need help?" Taliya asks as she eyes the familiar Amari, who is dodging with mixed success.

"Yes!" Wordlessly, the seer points to the roof access. A light enters the thief's eyes, and she grins before leaping off the edge of the roof. She flips mid-air to create momentum that sends her across the wide gap. Landing gracefully, Taliya darts to the roof access, lockpicks already out.

Amari turns her attention away just in time to see both familiars dive toward her. With a spike of panic, she throws herself out of the way and lands hard. Getting back up immediately, she starts a merry chase around the rooftops. It won't last long, she knows. Her stamina is fast running out while these creatures are built to last.

"Amari!" Taliya waves at her from the door, and the seer sprints full tilt in that direction. The gap is intimidating, and despite jumping as far as she can, she still needs the thief to catch her arms and pull her up.

Amari doesn't waste time catching her breath and runs for the door, familiars hot on her tail. They follow her inside the building despite its cramped space, and she sees an open window connected to a fire escape—smart planning on

Taliya's part.

The seer shoves through the window and nearly gives herself whiplash as she turns to close it with a loud bang. A sharp pain shoots through her brain, and Amari grits her teeth.

Both familiars screech their displeasure as they realize they can't follow her. One turns to leave the way they came, but Taliya closed and locked that door as soon as they passed the threshold.

This trap won't hold these creatures long. Amari and Taliya don't stick around to see it. They're a few roofs away when the girls are violently reminded that an archer is after them, too.

Another arrow comes, and Amari dodges toward it this time, rushing the assassin a dozen yards away. A nameless emotion is building in her, something finally starting to crack after days of intense moments.

It's a woman with stylish black clothes and antlers that signal her as an Andan. This only matters because the smaller size of the antlers indicates she is rather young.

Must be the Black Jay.

Surprised at the seer's sudden boldness, the assassin loads another arrow and aims for Amari's head. Her instincts warn her at the exact moment when to duck, and she slams into the Black Jay's torso with an angry tackle.

"What do you think you're—"

Taliya is right behind her, the knife she threw back in her hands, somehow. Her aim is deadly, nearly slashing Black Jay's throat if the woman didn't roll her and Amari out of range. The seer hisses and head butts Black Jay with her horns.

Most of the blow hits the antlers, but she smacks the woman's head, too, and briefly stuns her.

Amari is about to punch her lights out when her power spikes and her eyes dart to Black Jay's hand. Something small sits in it.

Grenade.

"Here we go," Taliya mutters as she hauls Amari up with amazing strength and pulls them over the side of the roof. They fall a story before the thief grabs onto a windowsill with one hand. She lets go, and they drop again until she uses another ledge to hold. Taliya's fast thinking and reckless movements are the reason she and Amari are out of range as the grenade goes off.

The sound of the explosion echoes in Amari's ears like a death knell, and for a moment, she's back in her vision. She tastes ash in her mouth and smells everything *burning*.

Thankfully, this explosion is rather small in comparison to what she saw. The building's structural integrity is still intact and everything.

"Alright, let's move," Taliya says. Amari realizes she's just hanging uselessly in the thief's other arm and quickly starts climbing the rest of the way down on her own.

"Is your arm okay?"

"Oh, yeah, fine. I've done worse drops with heavier loads," the thief claims cheerfully, to the seer's disbelief.

She doesn't say any more until they're streets away from the building, wary of any more tails. They are much more conscious of stealth going forward, even as Taliya seems largely unfazed by what just happened.

"That was wild! Can't believe you just bull-rushed her at the end!" Taliya sounds impressed and delighted, like some kind of lunatic.

All the while, Amari is clenching her fists and scolding herself internally. Losing her temper and being impulsive? She should have known the assassin would have insurance.

Sloppy. Stupid. Silly little—

"Hey, you alright?" Taliya is looking at her strangely, likely because Amari has been acting like a maniac.

"Fine."

"... Sure," the thief replies, an eyebrow raised. "Y'know, you're even weirder than I thought. This team-up was a great idea."

"That's what you're thinking? Really?"

Taliya shrugs, smiling wide enough to show sharp teeth. "Hey, I don't do well with people who are boring. You're just the right amount of over-prepared and reckless."

Her words drag a startled laugh out of Amari, surprising herself. "Shut up. I almost got us blown up."

"Not boring, like I said."

"I'm really starting to regret this team-up now," she snaps half-heartedly. Taliya must sense how little Amari means this because all the thief does is grin back. "Whatever. Let's just get out of here before we're ambushed again."

"Alright. Maybe use the scarf to hide your markings for now."

Amari grumbles as she does just that, covering her nose with the soft material. Some markings still peek out, most notably the crescent moon shape on the right side of her face. Plus, her ram horns and eyes are a bit of a giveaway, but the concealment helps. It eases her nerves, at least, as they continue the journey to the informant.

"I don't think they know about the break-in at the foreman's house yet or could connect us so soon," Amari speaks up as they travel across roofs. Taliya leads her across small jumps and narrow spaces with confidence in every step. The thief's balance never wavers for a second, and she seems sure of every place she sets her feet.

"Yeah, they're just after you," Taliya agrees. "I'll probably get a chance to explain since the sky bastard wants me in his gang. But if I refuse again, he'll try to have me killed."

Gritting her teeth again, Amari leaps over a wider gap between buildings and lands with bent knees to absorb the momentum. "All the more reason to cut him off here and now."

It takes less than ten minutes to reach the informant's 'place of work,' as Taliya calls it. The building is discreet, something Amari would walk right by any other day.

The Absent Ship is displayed on the storefront. They approach the bar together, sharing a nervous glance before leaving any uncertainty behind. The thief opens the door and walks in like she owns the place, while Amari follows at a more sedate pace.

Inside, the bar is slightly nicer than its exterior, but only barely. The place doesn't have much in the way of lighting, which feels rather nice on Amari's eyes after all that time under the sun. She recalls Taliya mentioning that this informant, Mia, is supposed to be a Nightblood, too. Will she even be awake and working right now? Evening is only about to begin.

What few patrons are there mind their own business, barely sending the two girls a second glance. Amari scans the occupants anyway, ever-present paranoia turning in her mind. Two men at the bar in hushed conversation, a small family eating at a table, and a blonde with electric blue eyes who gives Amari an amused look after the seer is caught staring. She dwells on them all briefly before dismissing them.

Taliya sits down at a booth, picks up a menu, and scans it with interest. Raising an eyebrow, Amari hesitantly takes a seat next to the thief. The other shrugs carelessly in response. "What? I'm hungry."

Thinking it over, Amari quickly realizes that she, too, is fast approaching starvation. The apartment was stocked solely with nonperishable food, and the menu features eye-catching pictures. "Alright, fine."

Honestly, Amari is grateful for the break. Her head is dangerously close to a full-blown migraine, and she briefly stops channeling any magic to the hearing enhancement runes.

Was it always this overwhelming? Does Amari just need to condition herself to noise again, or is this different? She feels like she's forgetting something, but is quickly distracted by the arrival of food they ordered.

They eat while waiting for the informant to show herself. Amari senses the moment the first moon is fully risen, and only has to wait a few more moments for the other Nightblood to appear.

Her eyes are bright red against the black sclera and white pupils, instantly zeroing in on Taliya, then Amari. Mia does not seem much older than them, but could more easily pass off as a young adult. Maybe eighteen or seventeen. The seer can admit to being impressed that someone so young can be an already infamous informant in Castor.

Taliya catches sight of Mia and waves her hand in greeting. The informant beelines for their table without pause, and Amari internally sighs before channeling a sliver of magic to her hearing enhancement runes. Just enough so she can easily catch the informant's words.

Up close, she's taller than the average Nightblood—who runs shorter than most other humans—and dressed in a way that suggests she has concealed weapons to Amari. Her horns curl around her head and are maroon, while Mia's markings crisscross her face in simple lines and patterns. Amari can't place their origin, not that tracing a Nightblood's marking is *easy* when there are so many options. It's why her patterns don't immediately give her away as a seer.

Mia grabs the back of a chair and drags it a short distance to their booth. She turns it backward and plops down in it, resting her marking-covered arms on the back as she peers at the two younger girls. "So, you're here to meet me, or is this just a coincidence?"

Right to the point. Amari likes her. Mia's voice is softer than the thief's, yet it contains a sharp edge to it.

"First one," Taliya says as she takes a bite of her sandwich. The smell of fish is a bit strong for Amari, and she's been fighting the urge to wrinkle her nose the whole time.

The informant hums, turning her head to watch Amari. It takes great effort not to fidget under the perceptive stare.

"Who's your friend?"

"My name is Amari Kato," Amari cuts in, not wanting Mia to get the impression that Taliya answers for her. She can speak for herself. "We're here to give you information and ask you to strategically spread it."

"Oh? Sounds important," Mia looks at the seer like she can see right through her, and Amari holds back a shiver. "Stuff like that will cost you."

"We can pay with more information," Taliya says, finishing off her food and wiping her hands. Amari ignores the rest of her plate to focus on the conversation.

"That'll do, depending on it being good info," Mia waves a hand, smiling pleasantly. Amari is reminded of a spider waiting at the center of a web and shifts in her seat uncomfortably.

Glancing around to ensure no one is looking, Amari pulls out a copy of the files from her bag. She and Taliya had decided earlier on the most significant documents to give to Mia. Now, Amari hands them over with trepidation.

The seer cleans up her plate as Mia goes through the file. Each document is carefully scanned and neatly organized into piles that Amari imagines have some relevance to the informant. She wants to ask, but holds back. Finally, Mia recollects the file and puts it in her comically small pocket. The magic is so blink-and-you-miss-it that Amari nearly convinces herself she mistook what she saw.

Mia must have worked magic similar to Taliya's bag into her own clothes. That is so... amazing. Amari wants twelve of those jackets.

"Alright, this is pretty big. The Rooftop King is expanding with the backing of a guild leader, which makes the chances of a gang war high."

"We'd like to curb those chances, if possible," Amari says, trying to appear more—she's not sure, authoritative? No. Maybe pragmatic?

"We'd like to crush them," Taliya crashes through, grinning widely. "Fuck the sky bastard, he'll bring the whole of the Upper's guards down on our heads."

"Yeah, no way this wouldn't get bloody," Mia sighs and runs a hand through her hair. "What is your plan, exactly?"

Deciding to follow Taliya's example of being blunt, Amari answers. "We want you to leak the information about the Rooftop King's guild leader to rival guilds. If they take care of one of their own crossing the line, that takes the gangster's backer out."

"Ooh," Mia bares her teeth at the idea. "I know *just* who to tell. The guilds aren't any better than the gangs when you get down to it. They're just better at appearing legit to the government and to the public. But they're all about their rivalries. This will cause *waves*."

"The kind of waves that don't kick-start gang wars, right?" Amari asks, feeling a little unsure.

"Nah, rich people are more likely to call on people like Taliya or do some contrived legal action that buries their troubles in bureaucracy. It won't be great, but it will be less outright violent for the Lower District."

"And the Rooftop King?" Taliya points out. Mia pats the pocket where the file disappeared into.

"Y'know, your information brings a lot of the stuff I've been hearing lately into perspective. The *king* has been sinking a lot of money and time into this project. If something were to sabotage it, he would lose more than just what resources he's invested. He could stand to lose everything."

Amari straightens abruptly in the booth, eyes widening. "What?"

"Oh, yeah," the smile on Mia's face can only be described as *schadenfreude.* "He's been making promises he won't be able to deliver on. To everyone in his gang and to outsiders, too. He'll have enemies up and down the coast."

"That explains why he's been so desperate to go after a single eavesdropper," Taliya comments idly. "And willing to kill me in the crossfire."

That's not particularly comforting. This makes it all the more important for Amari to seem *unimportant* again. She misses the days when no one spared her a second thought, despite those days literally being seventy-two hours ago.

"Here's the thing," Mia starts, and Amari narrows her eyes. The seer has been waiting for this whole conversation for the other shoe to drop. "I can handle spreading this information to the right people, but I can't do everything."

"What do you want?" Amari asks bluntly, not keen on talking around the subject.

"I *want* you both to break into the gangster's base and sabotage his magic supply. He's got a stockpile of power he's just sitting on for the day he wants to cause some real damage. That needs to be gone when I start messing up his project," Mia explains in a hushed voice, glancing around momentarily as she says this. "If you do this, consider your favor paid for. I have no love for the Rooftop King."

Taliya grins, not phased by the request at all. "Perfect."

"Hold on," Amari gripes. She feels like the only one with any sense at this table. "We need to know more than that before agreeing to something so dangerous. What kind of stockpile?"

"Tokens that store pure magical energy, which can be used to power virtually anything. There's also an armory of enchanted weapons and his horde of familiars."

The seer flinches minutely at the mention of the blasted creatures. She had been hoping never to see them again. "Are you serious?"

"As death. You make his magic supply useless, and the Rooftop King is finished. He'll be forced to flee Castor to escape all the people out for his head."

It's tempting. Too tempting, truly. One look at Taliya tells Amari that the thief is already on board with the idea. She has to grapple with herself for a moment, weighing the odds and whether the risk is worth the reward.

"... Fine. Tell us everything you know about the Rooftop King's headquarters."

Amari ends up spending the rest of the hour planning another heist, internally debating when she lost all her self-preservation instincts.

She goes home that night and only lets Taliya escort her to the general neighborhood.

"Nothing on you, but this is where I sleep," Amari says, feeling a little bad considering Taliya had taken the seer to one of her safehouses. Taliya shrugs, unbothered.

"No big deal. Meet you on the same roof as last time in 24 hours?"

"Yeah."

Left on her own, Amari makes the perilous yet familiar journey to her little haunted shack. The door opens for her before she can shove it forward, and she thanks the ghost with half her attention focused on her arm.

Runes have a varying level of permanence depending on the material they're written on. Human skin is a pretty temporary medium, so Amari has only a few weeks with the ones on her arm before they fade. She needs to memorize them so well that she can apply them to herself with her eyes closed.

However, the past day has been surprising. Amari had asked Taliya for the hearing enhancement runes as soon as the idea came to her, so she hadn't really gotten to consider what it would *be* like. Useful, she was sure.

The overwhelming feeling shocked her. Amari stopped putting energy toward the runes as soon as she left Taliya, and the relief was instant.

She needs to make a plan on how to condition herself to them. And practice with languages. It had been draining on her mental energy to listen and translate the conversation with Mia.

Amari starts making a list.

But something is still bothering her. It's like a thought just out of reach, something—

A sharp ache splinters through Amari's brain, and she hisses in pain. Her hands go to her head like that will stop the familiar sensation of an oncoming vision.

It's not too intense, thankfully. Amari doesn't even see anything. Instead, the taste of ash nearly chokes her and the smell of a city burning scorch her nose. Squeezing her eyes shut, Amari curls up into a ball on her bed as the sensations come in waves.

The echoing sound of screams rings in her mind, and Amari hastily builds her mental shields against the psychic incursion. Yet, when it comes to vision, shields only work so much.

It's a while before the pain passes, and so with it go the impressions of a city in flames. She almost wishes she could have just *seen* the thing instead of having every other sense assaulted like that.

Amari stays curled up, having no energy to move.

She gets the idea, okay? Castor is in danger. Her seer powers don't have to torture her with the knowledge.

Blinking her eyes open, Amari realizes her hands are covering her ears. The sound from the vision is purely psychic, but...

Oh.

Amari remembers now.

Hot tea at her bedside. A warm towel over her eyes. Ear muffs on her head.

That's what her mom would do for Amari after a bad vision. Everything would get overwhelming, and she couldn't process things as well at such a young age. Not that it gets much easier.

It was worse, then, wasn't it? Or... had Amari's hearing left her overloaded? She's always been a natural at telepathy and picks up things that most people miss. Her mental shields are better now, but it's not like Amari has to deal with a regular onslaught of background noise, does she?

Memories of reacting badly to too much sound unbury themselves, and Amari sits up with a start. As a kid, she had gotten overwhelmed easily.

How the hell had she forgotten that?

Trauma does funny things to the brain. A passage from a book surfaces in her mind. *Memories get twisted and warped with time.*

A subtle panic that has nothing to do with what she remembered comes over her.

Amari is the last seer. If she forgets, what's left? The thought hollows out her gut and leaves her breathing shaky.

She spends the whole night hunched over her notebooks, writing down everything she can remember about the seers. By the time the sun is up, she all but collapses in exhaustion and wakes up hours later feeling better than she has in years.

As the moons rise, Amari and Taliya are back on the same roof as before, giving them a clear view of Spirehaven's main headquarters. Once she woke up from some needed sleep, the seer gathered supplies for the second heist. She hopes she doesn't have to use them.

After some careful thought, she also keeps her hearing enhancement runes on a very low setting. Enough to easily channel more magic through if she needs to, but not enough to give her a headache.

"All ready?" Taliya whispers to her. The thief is dressed in clothes that look innocuous yet are easy to move in, the same as their last heist. This night, however, there are more obvious upgrades. Like the six smoke bombs strapped across her chest and the various knives sheathed within easy reach.

"Subtle," Amari notes.

"Oh, we've left subtly behind. This is a *real* heist."

The timing of the break-in is the most essential part of the plan. Between her and Taliya, they can pack quite a punch, but fighting a whole gang is out of the question. Fighting the

Rooftop King himself is a no-go as well, considering one of the reasons he's retained his position so long is through pure magical ability. They need to hit the gang's base when the leader isn't home, and it's at its most vacant.

The headquarters is a busy hub of criminal activity in the daytime, making the night the optimal time to sneak in. Nightbloods make up most of the human guards out now; thankfully, there aren't many of them. Amari counts only three on the main roof. Quite honestly, she's more concerned about the familiars. They populate various perches around the roof, some watchful while others nap.

Their greatest boon, however, is that the Rooftop King himself is away on business for the next few hours. According to Mia, he's conducting negotiations with smugglers on the other side of the river.

"It's time," Amari says, mostly for her sake. The seer's nerves are attempting to break her carefully maintained composure. It is better to forge ahead while she can still force herself. Taliya, showing no evidence of any such nerves, cheerfully starts to parkour in the direction of the headquarters.

Amari sizes up the tall building with a wary eye as she follows at a slower pace with much less flipping involved. The main base has many floors, but they only need to focus on the top two. With how heavily warded they are, getting inside through the ground floors is too much work. They're practically boarded up against entry. Everyone in the gang enters the building through the roof access, which makes it the least hostile to newcomers.

The top floor is used as a barracks and training area, but there's also an armory on Amari and Taliya's list of places where their objective might be. Second floor from the top is the Rooftop King's personal space, with the addition of a vault. Amari is hoping they find and destroy what they need to without going there. That's sure to be the most secure place in Spirehaven.

There are a few walkways between this building's roof and others, but Taliya and Amari don't bother using them. Instead, they scale the actual building while avoiding windows. It makes what would be a simple climb any other time something very anxiety-inducing.

Yesterday, on the walk to Amari's neighborhood, Taliya had explained this idea to the seer, who was rightfully very cautious. "That sounds like a great way to get caught."

"No, no, I've been getting around their security for years. I have a back door in the runework, so we won't be recognized as intruders by the exterior wards."

"... And the interior ones?"

"Well, those are more complicated. I need to work on those in person."

A canopy covers half the roof, so the two teens sneak in through one of the open spaces of the hub. Their bodies are strategically hidden from sight by a pile of crates—the storage area still being unloaded from a busy day of trade. One Sky Lord periodically comes and picks up a crate, so they have to time their entrance for just when the man is leaving.

On the roof, three Nightbloods remain as guards with a host of sleepy familiars. One of the creatures yawning nearly makes her startle. If she's this jumpy now, Amari can't imagine how nervous she would be if it were broad daylight.

They need to get to the end of the canopy that houses the Rooftop King's throne, which will require them to move out in the open. Thankfully, the two thieves have a plan.

Castor City's water system in the Lower District is notoriously bad. The filters aren't kept up to date or powered with enough magic. Anyone who can afford to buy clean water does. This means there are jugs of water stacked conveniently close by.

Amari cringes at the waste of water but nods to Taliya to start the distraction. Quietly, the thief begins singing under her breath, well-trained in channeling magic through her voice while staying unnoticed.

Water in the jug shakes at first, then one tip over and starts rolling. It looks like a natural domino effect, and the closest guard makes a noise of alarm before chasing after the runaway jugs. Another goes to help, while the third stays on watch on the other side of the roof.

Amari watches the familiars closely. The scene draws the attention of many and wakes up quite a few. However, they must all be comfortable with the busy nature of the hub, so once no threat is found, they all settle down.

"Now," Amari signs, and they dash for the canopy. It's only a few seconds where they're in the open, but it feels like a small eternity. Once they're firmly under the canopy's shadows, it becomes much easier to hide while still moving toward the throne.

It's as overly theatrical as she imagined it would be.

The Rooftop King's throne is at the far end of the King's Court, beneath the highest point of the canopy. It looks appropriately dramatic and ridiculous to Amari, who feels the man deserves a place in the theater. Fashioned from scavenged materials like ornate wrought-iron railings, splintered wood, and polished shards of broken glass, it looks menacing. The throne is raised on a dais made of cracked stone tiles, offering the King an unchallenged view of the entire court and the sprawling city beyond. Amari can't help rolling her eyes as she takes in the scene. Taliya actually scoffs, so at least she's not alone in her disdain.

More importantly, the roof access is behind it, with stairs leading down to the next floor. The seer follows the other's lead since she knows Taliya has been here before for work. Inside, the building is rather plain, with concrete walls and bare-bones decorations. Amari knows the King's area will probably differ and holds back the urge to sneer at the stairs leading further downward as they enter the top floor hall.

The hallway has four doors, and Amari mentally brings up the map Taliya made. One door is for the armory, and the other three are for the barracks, training area, and kitchen. Second door on the left is the armory. Amari decides to head directly for it, but the thief stops her with an outstretched arm.

"Wait," Taliya signs with an urgent motion. "There are some traps on the armory door. We need to steal a badge from one of the gang."

Amari is already grimacing as she lifts her hands. "One of the... *sleeping* gangsters?"

"Yep."

"Great."

Taliya walks up to the last door in the hall, softly inching it open to peek inside. After a moment, she swings it all the way and motions for Amari to follow. There's another hallway on the other side of the door, but she knows this one is for the dorm-like rooms the gang members share.

Amari's foresight kicks in as the thief reaches for the handle of the closest door. She gets the briefest flash of a man reading a book with a dim light and lurches forward to grab Taliya. Ignoring the flare of pain between her eyes, she grits her teeth and shakes her head.

"Not that room," Amari gestures emphatically at the other's confused look. She scans the hall, feeling out which dorm would be best. The third room on the right is what she ends up pointing at.

Taliya is side-eyeing her, and for good reason, but listens to her advice. It's a level of trust that Amari takes a minute to process fully. When she does, she has to swallow the sudden lump in her throat and shake off her surprise to focus on the heist.

The thief is in and out within a few seconds, having easily swiped a badge off a slumbering gangster's bedside table. She shows it off to Amari with a smirk before skipping back out to the main hall. Shoulders trembling with silent laughter, the seer follows as Taliya uses the badge to open the armory's door.

It swings open without a fuss, revealing a large room stocked entirely with enchanted weapons. Amari's mouth goes dry at seeing so many blades, bows, and cannons in one place. How can a gang have this kind of inventory?

Taliya whistles lowly, looking more impressed than disturbed. "More than I expected."

"Are the tokens Mia mentioned here?"

"I need to check those chests," Taliya points to the back corner of the room that has more weapons packed away than on display. Storage, Amari surmises.

She notices belatedly that the thief doesn't move after signing this. "... What's wrong?"

"Traps," Taliya snaps out quickly, waving at the whole room. Amari sees nothing inside that could be tipping the other off, but doesn't question her judgment.

"Alright, what do you need?"

Taliya eyes her, expression thoughtful. "You can sense danger or something, right?"

Tension wracks Amari's frame, and she holds onto her calm by the tips of her claws. She debates playing stupid, except she knows how insulting that would be. "... Yeah?"

"Can you point out the exact spots where the weapons will come out? I don't know how to dismantle this trap, but if you know what direction the attack will come from, I can dodge it."

Clenching her hands into fists, Amari takes a deep breath and focuses on the inside of the armory. Her heartbeat is pounding so hard that she wonders if Taliya can feel it.

Unsurprisingly, the armory is a reservoir of danger. It's chock full of weapons. *But what is an immediate danger?*

Amari's eyes are drawn to well-hidden panels in the ceiling and walls. She points them out to Taliya, not looking at the thief directly. It's not like Amari straight-up admitted to being a seer, yet it feels like she has.

Heedless of any awkwardness or danger, Taliya, bafflingly, cartwheels into the armory. Amari watches slack-jawed as the thief maneuvers around a spear launching from a hidden panel in the wall and a ceiling's falling guillotine. Taliya moves past a spray of arrows like a dancer on a stage, not taking a single hit. It's more enchanting than any magic Amari knows.

"Wow," she whispers.

Taliya lands on her feet in front of the chests, traps tripped and scattered behind her. Not a scratch on her. She opens the locks on the chests with an ease Amari envies, and she decides then and there to have the thief teach her some useful skills when this is over.

Amari waves to get the other's attention and signs her question. "The tokens in there?"

"Hmm, a few," Taliya holds one up to inspect it before stuffing it in her jacket. "Not enough for Mia to be concerned over."

"Then the King keeps the lion's share close," Amari scowls, having her hopes of avoiding the next floor down dashed. Looks like they're not done.

The Rooftop King's personal floor is less mapped out. People are generally only allowed into that level's office. Taliya did tell Amari earlier that half the floor is reserved for the gangster's personal quarters. His office and vault are next door, across the hall from each other.

It's also disproportionately big compared to the other floor. Amari realizes that the Rooftop King merged two levels into one, so he had more room as she looks up at the high ceiling. There are rafters above, specifically designed for Sky Lords to use as a comfortable perch.

Reaching the bottom of the floor, she and the thief carefully check the first door on the right. Inside is a lounge area that reminds Amari of what she had seen in the foreman's parlor. Maybe they bonded over similar bad taste. Taliya dismisses the room quickly and heads to the door on the left.

When the seer gets a buzz of warning, she moves closer to peek over the thief's shoulder. Amari barely reigns in a gasp at what she sees.

It's an actual dungeon. A prison cell with empty enchanted chains and wards scribed onto every surface. She smells old blood and sweat, making her gag reflex act up as she pulls away.

"Creepy," Taliya comments loud enough for Amari to catch, not looking as viscerally disturbed. Amari tries to quickly collect herself as the other moves on. "That's the office, which I know for a fact has nothing all that great... Oh, here we go!"

Taliya stops in front of a metal door, the frame looking much more durable than anything Amari has ever seen.

"How do we get in? The badge?" The seer signs with hesitant movements.

"No, a random minion wouldn't have access," Taliya shakes her head and studies the door closely. Her hands move quickly as she sorts out her thoughts. "The Rooftop King does a pretty decent job of not over-relying on wards as their only security. I can't just break into this with my runica like the foreman's house."

Amari tilts her head in thought, not seeing anything about the vault entrance that screams high-level security. "What do you need?"

Reaching into her bag, Taliya grins and pulls out a black case. She carefully places it on the floor and flips it open. Inside is an array of tools Amari couldn't hope to recognize or explain. The thief carefully pulls out a vial of shimmering liquid with a grin.

"I need ten minutes of quiet," Taliya signs with calm confidence. "Make sure no one sneaks up on us?"

"Sure," Amari agrees easily. She would be doing that regardless.

In the end, it takes Taliya eight minutes by Amari's count. The thief has gear meant for listening to the vault's lock and countermeasures for any surprise traps being sprung. Apparently, the enchanted liquid in the vial lets Taliya replicate whatever biometrics the vault is keyed into, so she doesn't set off any intruder alarms. Once that equipment is set up, Taliya works on figuring out the vault's key manually. It swings open without fuss before the ten-minute mark.

Inside, a treasure trove of chests, files, and dubiously legal inventory sits neatly organized. Amari glances through the aisle of items with sharp eyes, dismissing anything that doesn't look like it contains magic tokens. That still leaves a lot of areas to cover in their search.

"Nice," Taliya mutters as she eyes a stack of gold bars.

"Let's focus on the tokens," Amari signs sharply, expression firm, then relents at the thief's eye roll. "You can grab whatever you want after."

"Oh, I definitely will," is the response, accompanied by a gleeful look as Taliya darts toward a particularly large chest. Since it might be where the tokens are kept, Amari doesn't comment.

The seer nudges her magic gently at the vault room, trying to see if her power leads her anywhere. Unfortunately, what she gets back is similar to the armory. There's too much danger—or generally significant items—in one spot for her to parse out something specific. Maybe if they were looking for an actual bomb, it would be simpler, instead of looking for tokens of pure energy that *could* be used as a bomb.

Her powers a bust, Amari quickly starts opening and inspecting every chest or box in close reach. Mostly, she finds more weapons, (likely pillaged) treasures, and files. A part of her wishes she had the time to go through whatever documents the gang leader hides in his personal vault, but they can't dawdle. Better to assume they have less time than they think.

"What is this?" Taliya murmurs loud enough for Amari to notice, and she turns to look at the small jewelry box the thief is inspecting. It looks innocuous except for the toxic magic it's draped in.

Amari grimaces as she feels the energy that wafts off the artifact, and it reminds her of the Kiyoshi Crater. "Get back, that's haunted."

"Oh shit," Taliya backs off instantly, giving the jewelry box a wary look. She raises her hand to sign, and they stutter briefly before smoothing out. "You sure?"

"Yeah. And it's hostile, too. You can't feel it at all?" To the seer, the magic reaching out to grasp and *claw* at anything living is a blatant danger.

"Nah, never been very attuned to that stuff. Just the ocean and scribing, you know?"

And blood, Amari doesn't add. "Sure."

"Anything else *haunted* in here?" Taliya grins lightly while her eyes are narrowed and her gestures quick. At least she's being cautious about *something.* The seer dips back into her magic, trying to sense if there's anything else quite as blatant as the jewelry box.

"That painting," Amari points to a small frame on the other side of the room. It depicts a ghastly battle scene she can't place. "And the sword mounted on the back wall. Stay clear of those."

"Don't have to tell me twice," Taliya signs with a lazy flick of her fingers. "Knew some idiot who got possessed once. It was gross."

Amari's eyebrows raise in surprise. Possession is rare. Most 'ghosts' are actually just imprints of strong magical signatures left behind. What could they have been possessed by?

"Was it at Kiyoshi Crater?"

"Nah, some rich creep kept all these haunted artifacts in his basement. I honestly wouldn't have agreed to help break into the place if I knew beforehand. Only one of us was stupid enough to start touching stuff, though."

"Ah..." Amari grimaces again. "Yeah, I don't want to imagine the kind of things a rich hobbyist could get their hands on."

"You do not," the thief nods, something part amused and part grim flashing through her eyes. She emphasizes the next signs dramatically. "Anyway, *tokens!*"

Amari blinks, having completely forgotten the point of the heist for a minute. She resists the urge to smack her forehead and quickly resumes her search.

It takes her nearly fifteen minutes to open a large crate of tokens, practically overflowing with magic. Amari honestly flinches back from how much energy is hitting her in the face now. She looks at the outside of the crate, realizing it has been warded to muffle the feeling of magic. Smart.

"Found it," Amari calls out, and Taliya abandons her aisle to come over, crouching next to her. The thief whistles in appreciation of how much pure power is packed into one chest.

"Mia was right. Dissolving the tokens' hold on this much magic without blowing us all sky-high will be tricky." Taliya signs with a grim frown and severe movements so she gets her point across.

Amari's vision flashes before her, sending a shiver down her spine. Castor is in flames, and this crate is the center of it all.

"One at a time would be the safest," She signs sharply. The seer breaths in, trying to calm her heart. Amari's hands are surprisingly steady considering the storm inside her. "But very tedious."

"I... might be able to set up something that can do that?" Taliya suggests, while she leans to inspect the runes on the crate. "These aren't just for containing the tokens. There are runes to manage their upkeep, too. I could reverse engineer something. Still take time, but it would be automatic."

So, they could tamper with the crate, leave it here, and let it safely undo all of the Rooftop King's hard work right under his nose?

"I like that plan."

"I'll do that, then. You want to search the personal quarters?"

Amari wrinkles her nose in distaste and agrees to the task despite herself. Going into the gang leader's living quarters would be the last thing she wanted to do if the idea of leaving something unfinished didn't rankle her more. So, searching the Rooftop King's place it is.

The wards on the door leading to the living quarters are an immediate problem she solves by using her seer abilities to wardbreak. Taliya makes it look easy and systematic, while Amari is more like a drunk toddler with only a vague sense of where to draw in the lines. She's lucky she doesn't get vaporized. It works well enough if she doesn't count almost being cursed into a coma. Twice.

Inside, the gang leader clearly hoards all the excess he can afford for himself. Every meter of space is cleaner, newer, and more embellished than outside the living quarters. Her eyes glaze over fancy furniture and art in the foyer. Wandering through, she discovers a custom kitchen, an entertainment room, bedrooms, and more. All the while, nothing that looks like it's hiding more tokens jumps out.

Until she remembers the foreman's house and starts checking less obvious locations. Amari looks behind paintings, under furniture, and in the higher spots custom-made for a Sky Lord. She finally finds a chest behind a panel in an office and scowls when it's too heavy for her to drag to the vault. With it covered in wards, she's wary of opening it on her own and goes to get Taliya. At least it's much smaller than the crate.

"You done?" She waves to get attention and signs at the thief in the vault, still crouched next to the larger supply of tokens.

"Yeah," Taliya replies with a theatrical flick of fingers. "I've been tampering with these runes so they can't explode. They'll leak ambient magic slowly while remaining unaffected by their environment. The Rooftop King couldn't make these implode if he tried."

A great deal of tension leaves Amari's frame. "That's good. This is the lion's share. It could have probably taken out a few blocks or more."

She's understating things, obviously.

Taliya grins for some reason. "Yeah, that would be unpleasant."

Rolling her eyes, Amari steps back into the hall before freezing.

"What?" Taliya signs as the thief shows up next to her and raises an eyebrow at her.

"We need to hide," Amari is telling Taliya without any context. She surprises herself with the sudden message, but is already in motion before she has time to question it. The vault door is closed and locked in a moment. Her urgency takes her to the private room's threshold, and she closes it to avoid revealing the obvious break-in.

"I'll reactivate the wards," the thief signs with a reassuring quickness, working on the door after catching on to the sense of danger without question. It's a nice change of pace, the seer realizes, even as she is overwhelmed by her power's warning.

Something is wrong. Amari feels it in her bones. They have their end goal in sight and obstacles subverted, yet she has the creeping sensation that *something is wrong*. She's left in the gray space between panic and planning for what's coming without a clear reason. How can she plan for things she knows nothing about?

As she thinks this, the stairwell doorknob starts to turn at the end of the hall. Amari scales to the rafters without further thought, the thief right behind her. The sound of the door slamming into the wall from such a strong force nearly makes her lose her footing and fall from her perch. Even Taliya startles and shares a look of alarm with her.

The silver lining is that it quickly becomes clear that their break-in is still unnoticed. The bad news is that the Rooftop King is home, and he's pissed off about something.

Storming into the hallway, he's like a tempest in motion. Actual wind swirls around him in short bursts of anger despite being indoors. With no runes or singing apparent, Amari can immediately classify the man as a Conjurer like her—someone who manipulates magic with only their will. She notes with a heavy heart that he's adept at wind magic as well as the rumored mind magics.

Carefully, Amari builds up her mental shields, hoping to go unnoticed, and quickly signs at Taliya to do the same. If they're lucky, the man won't consider wasting energy trying to search for the minds of intruders he doesn't know are there.

This is her first time seeing the Rooftop King, and she must admit he looks appropriately intimidating. His wings are his most eye-catching features, primarily brown with bright gold streaks that shine under the lights. The wings are big, too, stretching taller than an already tall man. It makes Amari want to shrink into the shadows and not come back out until he's gone.

His features are weathered by hardship and sharpened with cruelty. Dark hair slicked back and clothes custom-made, he looks just like how she imagined a wealthy gangster would. Amari wonders if that's on purpose.

"—don't care if you have to wake up the whole building! You get them out, and you get it done!" The Sky Lord bellows as he enters, speaking at a glowing gem set into a watch. "I want the new warehouse set up before the end of the day. Get someone to open the place for you."

Whoever he's talking to must give some quiet agreement because the gangster taps the gem harshly and cuts the connection off, causing the glow to fade.

Trailing behind him is a trio of stone-faced minions who don't react to their boss's temper at all. Amari wishes she had that kind of iron will. Her hands are shaking in her effort to remain quiet and still. Next to her, Taliya has a somber frown on her face.

"Useless," the Rooftop King mutters, and Amari only hears because he walks directly under their hiding spot in the rafters. To her relief, he doesn't glance up. Even Sky Lords forget to check above, apparently. Or maybe he's just secure in his domain.

He stomps into his private quarters, and his minions take up posts, standing guard without needing to be ordered. They're blocking every possible escape directly, and Amari would bet the top floor is now very, very awake.

"This is bad," Taliya signs sharply once the goons are not right below them.

No kidding, Amari thinks unhelpfully. Instead of sharing that thought, she sinks herself into planning mode. "You have a way out?"

"All our exits are covered by gangsters, now. We'll need a distraction to get out unnoticed."

Creating a distraction from the Rooftop King's rafters that doesn't reveal them seems unlikely. So, she disregards that idea entirely. Their exit will be loud.

Her thoughts are interrupted by the gang leader coming back into the hallway, looking somewhat calmer. He heads directly for the vault door, and Amari holds her breath as she waits for any signal that he's noticed the break-in.

Apparently, for all his magical prowess, the Rooftop King knows nothing about wards except how to pay for them. He opens the vault with oblivious confidence and enters the room. Amari watches in fascination as he orders his men to take boxes and crates out of the vault. Her heart jolts when the crate containing the tokens is carried, but not one of the gangsters notices whatever Taliya did.

Next to her, the thief looks unbearably smug.

New minions come to the floor to begin ferrying the items away. She's desperately curious about what's going on. Maybe she can figure out how to get her and Taliya out of this situation if she knows. Hiding in the rafters' shadows will only work for so long. They're lucky it's worked *this* long.

"—smuggle it in a boat if you have to!" Amari leans forward ever slightly to hear the Rooftop King talk harshly into the glowing gem again. She channels magic into her hearing enhancement runes so she can eavesdrop. "We need this at the new warehouse today. Word has it that new regulations are starting next week on the Upper's docks, so we're doing this *now.*"

He wanders out of range for her to catch more, but she doesn't need to. Pieces are falling into place. The Rooftop King is moving into a new space in the Upper District.

Will this mean the building they're in will no longer be the gang's headquarters? Amari turns the problem over in her head. Either way, the importance of sabotaging the remaining tokens weighs on her.

How can they finish their job *and* escape?

"Going unnoticed is no longer an option," she signs quickly.

Taliya eyes her curiously. "What are you thinking?"

"Moonwalking bear," Amari answers before she can sort her thoughts into something coherent for anyone who's not her.

"*What?*" Taliya's sign is very theatric.

"It means inattentional blindness. You'll see."

Taliya, it turns out, thinks her plan is just the right amount of daring and reckless. Amari isn't sure whether to take this as a good thing. What's important is waiting out the moving of crates, so the base is nearly empty. Unfortunately, the remaining gangsters are concentrated on this floor to protect the Rooftop King.

Amari slinks through the rafters silently, hugging the shadows, until she's poised above the entrance to the leader's private quarters. Then she throws three of Taliya's smoke bombs down the hall and drops herself on the man standing guard outside the king's door, using her small body mass as much as she can to bring him down. Smoke briefly covers her attack as the other guards yell in surprise. The man she's balancing on topples, and she hits him hard on the head to keep him on the ground. Throughout the hall, the rest of the guards react with shock and alarm.

Most importantly, Amari is no longer concealing her mental presence.

The door in front of her opens as every conscious guard in the hall rushes through the smoke and tackles her. She is pinned roughly, her face and horns digging into the floor. Her claws itch to sink into one of the arms holding her, but she ignores the urge. This rough treatment makes her thankful she left her bag with Taliya.

Some nonverbal signal happens outside of her vision, and she's suddenly being half-dragged, half-carried into the private living quarters. Her head is forced down by a large hand on the back of her neck until she's harshly shoved to her knees in the private office and made to look up. The room is almost overcrowded, with guards staring down at her, all standing around one person.

"Now, who," the Rooftop King looms in front of her and leans in with narrowed eyes, smiling in a way that bares his teeth. "Are you?"

Amari instantly feels the presence outside her mental shields and instinctively strengthens them considerably. The Sky Lord raises his eyebrows in surprise, his smile turning a touch less angry into something more intrigued. Behind him, a guard leaves the room, leaving four left.

"Nice shields for someone so young," he murmurs. Amari doesn't respond, and it doesn't seem like a question either way. The presence mounts a greater attack, trying to understand how the seer protects her mind. "Answer the question, thief."

It's all about visualization and will. Amari doesn't imagine iron walls because they hold no significance to her. A good mental shield is built upon layers of memory and emotion. An image that *means* something to her.

The attack explodes against her shields in a fury, and she sinks into her mind to weather it.

It's a stormy night, shadows playing tricks on the mind as fire weaves into the forceful winds. Amari is in her home, hiding under her bed as the foundations shake. She's clutching a blanket and a knife like they'll save her. Outside, everything rages on and on forever.

She is in the eye of the storm.

This is a construct. This is a memory.

Amari dares anyone to get through the hurricane outside. The wrath of a god is inevitable in the way all natural disasters are, and she will be the only one left standing.

Whatever storms the Sky Lord has in his mind doesn't stand a chance to her own.

In the present, the Rooftop King flinches back from Amari, and his eyes widen in shock before narrowing in anger. "Who *are* you?"

The room has changed a bit in her distraction. Some guards move in the background, but the Sky Lord's form blocks her vision.

"... Sir?" The lieutenant, posted behind the gang leader, steps forward. The Rooftop King waves his hand in acknowledgment instead of looking back. "She fits the description of the eavesdropper one of the familiars reported days ago."

"Oh, really? How interesting," he tilts his head to the side, and she can't get a proper read on the emotion crossing his face. Whatever it is, she's not optimistic about it. "Someone knows more than they should. Care to share?"

Amari keeps her silence for now. One of the guards walks forward, causing the lieutenant behind the king to look at them strangely.

"No? Fine."

A fist slams into her face and knocks her onto her back before she can finish her sentence. It stuns her briefly, and she spends precious seconds staring at the ceiling blankly before refocusing. The Rooftop King is standing, wings spread halfway to create a truly intimidating silhouette.

"I would say you'll regret this day for the rest of your life," he sneers down at her as she struggles to sit up. "But that won't be very long."

The guard opens his palm to her, showing a tincture and a token.

"Well, there's your mistake," Amari says through blood-stained teeth. "I didn't come to steal anything."

"What? What are you—"

He's cut off by an explosion, igniting and throwing both on their backs. Amari is expecting it and does her best to roll to her feet. The Sky Lord and his lieutenant slam into a wall, their wings protecting them from most of the damage.

That's alright. Amari isn't done. She looks to see the remaining guard pulling out the chest full of tokens with mechanical movements. Seeing them puppeted in real-time is rather eerie, especially since they aren't allowed to talk and give away the game. The seer glances up, sees nothing, and then goes to the door.

It's closed but opens a second later to reveal Taliya, who is humming quietly. Her vest has considerably fewer knives strapped to it, and wisps of smoke follow her.

The Rooftop King staggers to his feet, face awash with fury as he glares at the girls. *"Traitorous—"*

Without hesitation, Taliya dumps Amari's bag over the chest of tokens. Her stolen magic amplifiers fall out, the tinctures cracking open as they hit the tokens.

What happens when you mix a massive amount of energy tokens with concentrated magic amplifiers? Amari hopes they survive to find out. The slow realization that hits the Rooftop King is beautiful, and she savors the petty satisfaction that getting one over on him causes her. Victory is a rush.

"No," the gang leader says, disbelief in his voice with a growing undertone of horror. "You're insane."

"You should run," Amari smiles. "Better yet, *fly.*"

"You—"

Taliya sings a sharp note, catching the man's attention. A water pipe in the wall behind him bursts under sudden pressure and drenches the room. Wasting no time, Amari reaches for a grip on time and reaches for Taliya's hand. As soon as she touches the thief's skin, they're both in the seer's bubble.

Time is slowed around them, and the water from the blown pipe is still hitting the Rooftop King. The tokens are dissolving from too much magic, and Amari can see sparks beginning to appear. A dull roar of *danger* is building in the back of her mind.

She turns to Taliya, who's taking in the scene with a fascinated look. "Fastest exit?"

"Window," the thief answers without pause and drags Amari with her to the closest one. She opens it swiftly and gets onto the windowsill. The next roof over is a big jump, but it's also their only option. Behind them, Amari notices the gang leader starting to turn toward them. She hastens to join Taliya.

They push off the window simultaneously, yet Taliya is the one to make it to the next roof safely. Amari nearly falls if not for the thief's impressively strong grip. She's pulled up, and they dash across the rooftop—and keep running.

The sound of a bomb exploding in slow motion is not something Amari will soon forget. Neither is the building collapsing in on itself. She brings herself to a stop to look at the aftermath.

Her vision overlaps briefly, showing her how close Castor came to real destruction. Instead, one building is wrecked beyond repair. Finally, something in her uncoils.

The bomb's aftermath is beautiful in its devastation. It makes Amari's heart try to climb into her throat. The last time she saw something like this...

"That was... insanely risky," Taliya cuts off her train of thought with a grin as she pulls Amari to the edge of the roof.

"I know. Uh, sorry?"

"Don't apologize! I don't usually use that much magic, and I wasn't expecting it to be so tiring. Most fun I've had in months!"

"*Fun?* And you're calling *me* insane?"

"Like knows like and all that," the thief laughs as she bumps shoulders with the seer and lets go of her hand. Time normalizes with a loud crash as the building continues to experience the fallout from the explosion.

"You're ridiculous."

Amari sits down on the edge of the roof with a heavy sigh, head aching and limbs sore from all the last twenty-four hours' abuse. Her legs swing idly as her new... almost-friend plops beside her with an ease that belies Taliya's graceful movements.

Distantly, she can see past the Lower District to the water and onto the outlines of the rest of Castor. It's strange to think how much has happened since she was last on the other side of that river.

A ruckus in the streets below draws her attention, and they get the beautiful sight of the Rooftop King's gang scattering like rats. They'll soon come to find that not only is their main headquarters rubble, but their whole operation is going to fall like a deck of cards. Mia seemed delighted with the challenge of it.

"Good riddance," Taliya says, a sharp grin lighting her face. The braids framing her face sway gently in the wind, and Amari smiles.

"Want to go get some food?"

"*Yes,* I'm starving," the girl gets up smoothly and walks away from the scene of destruction with the same lack of hesitation she had starting it. "I know the perfect place. You won't believe the—"

Amari follows quietly, more at peace than she's felt in years.

Also by B.R. Michaels

Stolen Histories

By B.R. Michaels

More from the world of Avalon with Amari and Taliya!

About the Author

B.R. Michaels writes fantasy stories filled with creative worlds, eccentric characters, and humor while tackling real-world issues. They are a lifelong lover of speculative fiction, and they mostly spend their time holed up in their library or getting lost in bookstores.

When not writing, B.R. Michaels can be found watching comedy with their mom and playing with their dogs. Their work often explores themes of found family, moral ambiguity, and the cost of power, and they love crafting stories that blend adventure, heart, and a touch of the unexpected.

You can find them at brmichaels.com/home.

9 798992 598476